PLAYING WITH FIRE

SALLY PRUE

previously published as *The Devil's Toenail*

SCHOLASTIC INC.

New York Toronto London Auckland Sydney
Mexico City New Delhi Hong Kong Buenos Aires

ISBN 0-439-48635-1

12 11 10 9 8 7 6 5 4 3 2 1   5 6 7 8 9 10/0

Printed in the U.S.A.   40

First Scholastic paperback printing, October 2005
The text type was set in 12-point ACaslon Regular and AGaramond Italic.
Book design by David Caplan

1

"Go on, then."

There were five of them. The dusk had taken their color away so they were all bones and shadows: even Ryan, who had a face like a hamster's.

"What do you want me to do?" I said.

"It's got to be something difficult," said Jack, relishing it. "Something really funny."

Jack's idea of funny runs towards smashing bottles in the children's playground.

No problem.

But Daniel had a faraway smile on his face; and Daniel was clever. He knew things: especially the things you'd never told anybody.

"Something dangerous," said Daniel, gently, "and extremely entertaining."

Daniel loved long words, he enjoyed the taste; but no one made fun of him because he was really cool and good-looking.

Ryan rocked from side to side on his huge backside and sniggered happily. He was feeding a strip of toffee into his face. His shirt had channeled his fat into rubber-ring rolls.

I waited. I'd taken a lot of trouble to get in with this lot, and I wasn't going to throw it all away. I looked at Matt, but he was lying on his back next to Ben and seemed more than half asleep.

"Get him to nick something from one of the shops," suggested Jack.

Well, even *Ben* had nicked stuff from shops, and he was so small and weedy he was practically invisible.

I only hesitated for a moment — just thinking about it — and that was the moment everything went wrong. Just that moment. If I'd only just gone and done it straight away — nicked some chips or something — then it would have been all over. But there was just that little second of silence, and Daniel got into it. He was just so clever, Daniel was.

"No," he said. "Even someone from *Highford* could do that."

Yeah, OK, my parents sent me to Highford School because of its exam results. But then I got into trouble, and so I left, and I ended up at Farmstate. Me, from stuck-up Highford, at Farmstate.

It's a bit difficult.

Matt yawned and rolled over.

"This is boring," he said.

"Yeah," said Jack, who has the attention span of a flea-ridden gnat. "He's a prat from Highford. I bet he couldn't do anything anyway."

I fixed Jack with my eyes and did my psychopath face. I'm quite scary when I do that.

"Oh yeah?" I asked.

Well, you have to stand up for yourself, don't you?

But Daniel reached his hand into his pocket and took out a cigarette lighter. It looked solid gold.

"Go and set fire to the wastepaper bin in the library," he said.

That took us all by surprise.

"Only wimps go in the library," pointed out Matt, frowning.

But Jack laughed.

"It'd be really funny," he said. "We could wait outside and watch all the little old ladies and Highford prats running away."

He put his hands in the air and ran round in a circle squeaking, *Ooh, ooh!*

Everyone laughed, except me.

I stood there looking at the little gold box. Full up, it was, of stuff that flicked into flame so easily . . . the whole bin would go up in a roar. Hot. Ever so hot.

Suddenly sweat was running down one side of my face. And I got all confused. That happens, sometimes, when I'm in a group of people. And, you see, I don't — I don't *like* fire.

There. I've never told anyone that before.

Daniel was watching me, enjoying it.

"The library doesn't close for half an hour," he said, just so sleek.

But my heart was pumping, and I knew I couldn't do it. Just knew it, without any doubt at all. And there were all these faces round me, staring at me, and I didn't know what to do.

My bike was there. I never go anywhere without my bike. I got on it and felt a bit better. Jack was still tiptoeing round in circles, squawking; but Matt was looking at his watch.

"Don't do it now," he said. "I've got to be getting back."

Matt works at his dad's stall at the market. He makes really good money, but he has to get up at five every Saturday. Even when it's half-term break.

"Tomorrow, then," said Daniel. And he looked at me and he saw inside me and he was just loving it.

"I can't," I blurted out.

Jack let out a laugh like an anemic machine gun.

"He's chickening out!"

"No," I said, quickly, and for the first time ever I was actually grateful for my family. "But I'm going away on holiday tomorrow morning. I'll do it when I get back. OK?"

Ryan sighed contentedly: he was tearing open another strip of toffee and his face was so fat it had squeezed his mouth into a dimple only just big enough to take it. The last thing he wanted to do was waddle down to the library.

The holiday would give me a chance to get over my fire thing. Perhaps if I thought about it really a lot, so I sort of got used to it . . .

Anything could happen.

Daniel smiled, put his feet up elegantly on Ryan's mountainous belly, and no one ended up doing anything.

· · ·

I cycled part of the way home with Matt. He asked me where I was going on holiday, so of course I said I was going skiing in Austria with my uncle. It would have been better to have said with my dad's business partner, but I didn't think of that until afterwards.

"Cool," he said, as he swooped away past my turnoff and down the hill.

Yeah, it was cool: there I'd be, skimming through the pine trees — grim, fast, and handsome. Soaring off the jumps.

Is it a bird, is it a plane . . . ?

Yeah, cool.

But not, unfortunately, true.

2

My name is Clarke Connery.

Oh, all right, it isn't really, it's Steve. Stephen Geoffrey Saunders.

I wasn't going to admit to that, but I've decided to tell the truth, and I suppose that's part of it.

What else will you need to know?

Ah. Yes. Well — this is going to be really embarrassing, but you'll need to know about — well, about my family.

Right. OK, here goes: Mum and Dad — just the usual — Claire, aged six, pigtails, mixture of Genghis Khan, Vlad the Impaler, Tinkerbell, and a PE teacher.

Yes, that bad, really: a PE teacher.

But you know how it is. I mean, I can't *help* having a family. And they have nothing to do with me, really; I just live in their house. I mean, I'm out a lot.

"Have you packed some pajamas?" asked Mum.

"I don't need pajamas," I said.

"You will in the camper; it's all windows. Take those nice stripy ones Grandma bought you."

Yes, yes, all right, all right. We were borrowing Grandma's trailer camper and going to the seaside for the Bank Holiday weekend. I mean, *brilliant*.

Packing to go on holiday is horrible. It's Mum. She has this thing where we have to leave the house really clean, and it gets to the stage where she doesn't even like you going to the loo in case you splash.

No. This is all wrong.

Look, I've not done this sort of thing before, and it's hard to know what to put in. What's important. What needs to be there. Not that things make sense, anyway. Perhaps if I could start everything again — if only I hadn't done this. If only that hadn't happened. . . .

Dad came into my room to get my rucksack, heaved it onto his shoulder with a gargling groan, and limped heavily down the stairs. It's not that he's really got a limp, but being ill's one of his hobbies. That, and bird-watching.

Getting away from it all. That's what they say about holidays. If only. It all goes with you, in your brain, scratching and nibbling like little mice. Always there, always. Always.

8

Set fire to the library bin.
Set fire to the library bin.
Set fire to the library bin.

In the end we were packed — aspirin, matches, vegetable knife — and Dad had locked all the doors and windows and switched off all the switches, and gone back to check them, and gone back to check them again; and Mum had got all stressed because she thought the drain might be blocking up but there wasn't time to do anything about it; and Claire had gone round the front lawn and stamped on all the daisies; and then at last it was time for me to edge my way gingerly into the back of the car that was already filled up with Claire, four coats, and fifty-six Barbies.

And then Dad wrestled our rheumatic old car into gear and we were off to jolly old Grandma's to pick up the camper. And straight away — *oh, joy* — Mum and Dad started singing the theme to *The Great Escape*.

I suppose I could have thrown myself out of the car in front of a truck: but unfortunately Dad had the child locks on.

3

"Well, you should have left me at home, then," I said.

It was really hot. Typical, isn't it? We'd been freezing and drowning all year, and then the one day when we're banged up inside a tinny car for hours it turns out blistering.

Mum was fussing about sunblock and hats. I have my hair really short, and she pretends she's worried about sunstroke and skin cancer, but really it's a power thing.

"You know we couldn't leave you," said Mum. We were having lunch amongst the dog mess outside a service station and we were all sweaty and horrible. And Claire had said, *Are we nearly there yet?* fifty-six times already. "You're too young to be left, Stevie."

"But Daniel goes on holiday by himself," I said. "He went to Australia go-karting last year. Why can't we do good stuff like that?"

"I'm not interested in what Daniel does," said Mum, offended. Mum doesn't approve of Daniel because he got expelled from his last school.

By the time we'd finished lunch, the air in the car was thin with the fumes of heat-limp plastic. But off we went, on and on — *Are we nearly there yet?* — and it was boring and boring and boring.

The car was stifling, sticky, unbearable, but all of a sudden we'd turned off the grinding main road and that meant we really were nearly there. My skin was fused together with sweat, but despite that I began to feel this expanding feeling.

"Only five minutes now," said Dad.

"Just on time," said Mum.

Suddenly I was quite looking forward to it —

And then Claire puked all over everything.

Typical: I mean, really typical. She might have waited another five minutes. I wound down my window and leaned out while Mum and Dad scooped up vast quantities of slimy vomit into tissues and dabbed despondently at everything. Mum said we weren't to put our feet on the floor because it was splattered with sick.

Claire isn't my real sister: she can't be. I mean, I'm not even convinced she's human. I think she must have been swapped in her cradle by a family of ghouls who found her unsavory.

But then there was the sign, and we turned in, and we were there.

"Look!" said everyone. "The sea! The sea!"

4

What are holidays *for*? I mean, you drive for eons through wedged traffic, and then when you get there you have to find an empty square of grass, unhitch the camper, sort out the poles for the tent extension, fix it onto the camper, fetch the water, dig out Claire some non-puky clothes. And then it's time for Dad to have his traditional fight with the water heater, at which point anyone sensible gets the hell out of there. Well, if the water heater *is* going to explode, there's no point in us *all* getting burned alive, is there?

"Are you off for a walk?" asked Mum, as I slunk off. "Hang on, and Claire and I will come with you." But I managed to shut the door of the camper just in time so I could pretend not to have heard.

I dug my hands into my pockets and wandered aimlessly down through the rows of campers. There was no one much about, which was good. I like it best when there's no one about. Anyway, I went through an

13

archway by the pool and there it was. The beach. The sea. No one else — just the sea, and the beach, and me.

OK, it wasn't exactly Ibiza — let's face it, it wasn't exactly Clacton-on-Sea — not a single ice-cream van or stall selling inflatable crocodiles; in fact it was all jumbled stones and patchy bits of shingly sand. But I like beaches.

I walked along until my shoes started leaking, and then I climbed back up to the dump of stinking seaweed that marked high water and sat down. If you look really closely you can find all sorts of things. But you have to look.

The first things were shells, worn chalky by the sea; and then there was a big crab's claw that still worked; and a chunk of quartz-like Turkish delight. It glowed like broken fire when you held it up to the light, but it was cold. Really cold. Wonderful.

But then there was a shout that made me jump, and it was Dad. They'd followed me. Dad and Claire. And I wasn't by myself anymore. And everything was spoiled.

"There you are," said Dad, trying not to sound relieved. "Mum's just getting dinner ready."

I shoved all my treasures back on the beach and they disappeared again among the stones.

"You won't be long, Stevie, will you?" said Dad.

But I'd found an old aerosol can that had got tangled up in a heap of seaweed, and so he wandered off to where Claire was grubbing about.

Mum doesn't buy aerosol cans because they destroy the ozone layer: she's prehistoric. This one had a sign on the back that said HIGHLY FLAMMABLE. So I put it down again.

Claire had decided to push Dad into the sea. So Dad ran away, and Claire ran after him, and then I was alone again.

I started throwing stones.

It's great, throwing stones. Skimming them. I even got some to bounce, and that's not easy on the sea.

Pack up your troubles in an old black stone and smile, smile, smile.

I don't know where that song came from, but I found myself throwing stones in time with it.

While you've a lucifer to light your fire —

No.

Suddenly I'd had enough of the beach. Anyway, I was hungry. But as I pushed myself up my hand closed on one last stone, and I just happened to glance at it before I chucked it.

And I couldn't believe it.

I turned it over to make sure, and it was. It really was. Quite small: about one-and-a-half by one inch, domed, but narrower at one end than the other. And underneath it was a bit like a horseshoe: a U-shaped edge and the rest hollowed out.

Look, I can't describe it — it would take all day, and then you wouldn't have a clue. I'll draw it.

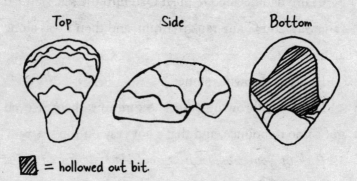

Top   Side   Bottom

= hollowed out bit.

Well — I hope you get the idea. I'm not much good at graphics. Obviously.

But anyway, I knew what it was. Dad had shown me and Claire one in a museum once, and the name had stuck in my mind.

It was a good name.

It was a devil's toenail.

5

I was just so surprised and pleased. I stood there, rubbing the devil's toenail with my thumb, gloating over it. I thought about how old it was and I wanted to jump up and down and hoot like a baboon.

I set off back to the camper, but I kept on getting the devil's toenail out of my jeans pocket so I could rub my thumb over the wavy ridges and gloat over it. And I felt — oh, I don't know — like someone who'd discovered a new planet.

OK, it wasn't really one of the devil's toenails: OK, it was just the fossil of a shellfish; but — well, it was a bit like all those ancient monuments. I mean, Stonehenge is only a few lumps of stone, but it's still got this dark power, hasn't it?

I read this book once — I had to, it was a school project — and it had all this stuff in it about ancient sites and the power they have. There was a bloke who

17

could feel it vibrating through him, and it made him go all dizzy and stuff.

And I thought that if I held the devil's toenail in my hand, and I looked at it, perhaps, really close so I got cross-eyed — and if I concentrated really hard, then maybe I'd pick up this dark power and . . . and it'd be just so cool.

Who are you?

And it was funny, but there *was* something a bit strange about the devil's toenail: it didn't feel quite like stones usually did. It was warmer, for one thing, and the ridges across its domed back felt sort of satisfying.

Stephen Geoffrey Saunders. Yes. Stevie.

And you believe in darkness.

And, what was really odd, when you'd had it in your hand for a little while it felt as if it was fizzing.

So what can I do for you, Stevie? What do you want? What's important to you? Wealth? Pleasure? Power?

Yes, there was a definite fizzing that spread up through your arm in a crackly electrical sort of way; and as it did, it was funny, but it made you feel strong. Yes, really strong and powerful. I mean, wow, it was great. And then the fizzing reached my stomach and I suddenly felt ten feet tall. I could have vaulted every wall and raced every car. It was like being Superman. Yeah, just like being Superman.

Superman? Well, not exactly, Stevie. More like Lex Luthor, really. But you'll soon find that out.

I didn't even bother about the crowd of dodgy blokes in the playground, because now I'd got my devil's toenail no one could do anything to me. I felt invulnerable, that was the word. Invulnerable and powerful and happy.

I will make you a new person, Stevie.

Real novelty, that was.

I got to the camper, leapt up the step, opened the door — and there was Mum, just serving up.

Watch out! She's the enemy. The enemy, Stevie. Don't listen to her. Believe in me and I will give you —

"Just in time, dear," she said. "Good boy."

And I had this feeling — *shrriiinnnk* — and I went from Superman to Stephen Geoffrey Saunders in two seconds flat.

And nobody even said, *Is it a plane?*

I mean, what a letdown.

Not that I *really* want to be Superman, obviously: well, it's just not cool, is it? I like to think I'm more like Lex Luthor, really — only with a bit more style.

Of course, Daniel's the one who's really got style.

He's incredible. We started at Farmstate on the same day, but if we hadn't been introduced to the class together I'd never have known, because even then you'd have thought he owned the place. All the girls were gawking at him as if he'd dropped from heaven.

Matt got lumbered with looking after us. Well, Matt was Most Popular Guy, you could see that; and Daniel shook his hand — yes, really — and everybody took it for granted that they'd be Best Friends because they were the Best People.

I liked Matt right from the start, but even on that first day Daniel would take him by the elbow and say things I couldn't quite hear; and already it was as if I was a bit of an outsider. But Daniel was just so cool, and Matt was just so nice; and so I hung around, like a spare part, until in the end, after weeks and weeks, Daniel said that if I wanted to be part of their gang then I'd have to pass a test. And he looked right inside me and saw that I didn't like fire; and so he said that I had to set fire to the bin in the library.

But they might have forgotten about that by the time I got home.

Daniel? Forget?

I was a bit worried about it all, to be honest. You know, because of my fire thing.

Claire kept trying to pinch my nose with a crab's claw she'd found on the beach. She really needed dismembering, did Claire.

"Don't do that, darling," said Mum. "Why don't you wait until after dinner and then you can pinch Daddy's nose."

Dad didn't hear — he's always at least six conversations behind. I mean, what a family. There was Dad, who inhabited some dismal part of outer space; Mum, who dedicated her life to attempting to live in an out-of-date sitcom; and Claire, enhancing our mealtime with her revolting smelly crab's claw. Dad shouldn't have let her bring rubbish like that back from the beach.

When I thought about it I could still feel the devil's toenail fizzing, even though it was in my pocket.

Yes, Stevie. You can feel my power.

And OK, I didn't feel ten feet tall anymore, but I still felt really strong — and I just wondered if I might be able to do things I hadn't been able to do before. I might even be able to set fire to the library bin —

OK, maybe not that. But I might be able to do

something else. Something so brilliant that the gang's eyes would pop out and they'd go down on their knees and beg me to join the gang.

So —

Just keep believing, Stevie. And doing what you're told.

So now I had to try it out.

6

The worst thing — the very worst thing, and this is saying a lot — the very worst thing about being on holiday with your family is the embarrassment.

You see I'm really tall — though, admittedly, I am only about an inch and a half wide — so I look older than I am. But what's the point of having shaved hair and cool clothes if you have to go round with your parents and a horrible little girl with a loud mouth?

The only thing that stopped me shriveling away completely into a blob of grease was that I had my devil's toenail in my pocket. Everyone might have thought I was just an ordinary pathetic boy trailing around after his parents. But really the fizzing power of the devil's toenail was simmering inside me and I felt strong. Really strong.

Weak people aren't worth knowing, Stevie.

When I think about it, I can see why you'd want to have a test for people before you let them into the gang.

You wouldn't want anyone pathetic in with you: not the kind of person who spends all his time talking about homework. Daniel only made Ryan do shoplifting for his test, but then Daniel said Ryan was too stupid to do anything better. I wish I'd seen it, though, because it must have been really funny. Ryan got his granddad's old raincoat, and he made some hooks from coat hangers that he hung on the band inside the waist. Then he was all set up. So he went into this eco-friendly shop in the Old Town that doesn't have everything wired to the shelves, and he got a couple of really neat solar-powered radios and hung them on the hooks inside his coat. He must have looked like an escaped tent.

It worked, too. It worked right up to the point where he went through the scanner by the door and set the alarm off.

Well, he scarpered, of course, but he runs like a chimp in flippers at the best of times so he didn't get far, particularly as he knocked one of the radios with his elbow and somehow managed to turn it on. So he didn't exactly merge into the crowd: he was the little fat one in the dirty coat with the orchestra blasting out of his belly.

Jack was there, with Daniel, watching, and he said it

was the funniest thing he'd ever seen. Apparently even the shop manager had trouble keeping a straight face. And the police nearly wet themselves laughing.

So Daniel let Ryan into the gang anyway, for entertainment value, despite the fact that he was so fat and smelly. Well, Ryan *was* funny: he was so stupid he'd do anything Daniel said, and Daniel got really crazy sometimes.

Right. Where was I? Oh, yes. Shuffling my way out to the car through the morning sunshine. It was England, and it was the beginning of summer, but it was really baking, blinding hot. Which would have been good, I suppose, except that Dad was insisting on keeping his coat, scarf, and gloves on because he thought he had a touch of pneumonia.

What do you expect, Stevie? He's family, and families are dangerous. They warp your mind. Keep away from them.

I went on ahead and tried to look like someone old enough to live by myself.

Remember that, Stevie: families ruin you; they scrape your life to the bone.

The thing about holidays is that we all hate them. All Dad wants to do is go bird-watching: but he hardly ever gets the chance because the rest of us get bored. And Claire screams all the birds away anyway.

"There's this nature reserve —" began Dad, who never stops hoping.

"I want to go to the beach," announced Claire, loudly and firmly, from under her lime-green elephant hairband.

"We'll have to find a supermarket," said Mum, all crumpled shorts and white wobbly legs. "That might not be easy on a Sunday."

"I don't know why you couldn't have left me at home," I said.

And so of course we compromised, which is what we always do unless Claire's actually biting pieces out of our kneecaps, and we ended up going somewhere none of us wanted to go.

Except me, Stevie.

7

It was a little seaside town with narrow streets and one-way signs and nowhere free to park. We found out there was nowhere free to park by driving round and round the town for twenty irritable minutes. Dad always does that because he won't ask for directions. It's quite funny, because Mum gets so uptight. And in the end, the final end, when Mum was about to whimper and beg to go home, we ended up in a car park and discovered they were all free anyway because it was still the off-season for parking.

Well, Dad took himself off to the seawall to look at the seagulls, and that left me trailing round after Mum and Claire. You can guess how it was.

Gift shop.

Gift shop.

Gift shop.

And, guess what next?

Yes, a gift shop.

Of course Mum was fully occupied saying, *No, Claire, I'm afraid it's too expensive,* or *No, Claire, we haven't got room in the camper for a rocking horse, have we.*

The shops were full of crap — pink bucket-and-shovel sets, and dusty shells, and souvenir crocheted toilet-roll holders that weren't even worth *nicking*.

And then something happened. Have you ever walked under electricity pylons? Because it was something like that: hair-lifting and skin-prickly — but sudden, really sudden. And there I was, alone, in the dimness at the back of the shop.

There was a glass cabinet full of knives there.

So shiny, aren't they, Stevie? So delectable.

I looked at them. They were turning round in one of those little spotlight things, and they were just so classy. Some of them had zillions of extra things on them: scissors, screwdrivers, things for getting stones out of horses' hooves. Not that you'd get me anywhere near a horse, but then you never knew.

And I really wanted one. The big shiny red one. Yeah. I mean, you have to take care of yourself, don't you?

It's only right that you should have it, Stevie.

I wanted that knife, suddenly, in a way I'd never

wanted anything before. The red handle shone at me promisingly, beguilingly: and my heart was beating fast.

Taking things from shops is really easy. You have to be as ham-fisted as Ryan or Jack to get caught. I mean, *I've* never been caught, not once. You just have to keep an eye out for mirrors and tags and shop assistants, that's all.

It's not even wrong, is it, Stevie? It's just making things fair.

And at least there is some *point* to shoplifting. Not like pulling the wings off fledglings, which is the sort of thing Jack enjoys.

I looked round. Claire was admiring a witch's hat, and the woman at the cash register had been in a trance ever since we'd come in. Jack's always saying you can open these display cases really easily with any key you happen to have on you — and I never go anywhere without the key to the padlock for my bike.

I glanced round again, really casually. No one else in the shop. That was good because I feel more comfortable when there aren't too many people about. I got out my key. It looked about the right size. OK. OK. One more casual glance around.

And everything will go according to plan, Stevie.

The electricity was all round me now, and I suddenly felt as if no one could see me. Everything was all right. Right. Nothing to stop me. Nothing at all. Coast completely clear. And —

The alarm hit me like a punch in the face. I swear I nearly knocked myself out on the ceiling. And Mum and Claire and even the catatonic shop assistant were looking at me. Looking at me.

My plan, anyway.

I hate it when people look at me. And I was suddenly hot and burning and I couldn't breathe, couldn't see. And I was blundering away, out of the shop and out into the cool air. And Mum was making yapping noises behind me, but I wouldn't stop, out of the dim shop with the alarm going on and on and on, like the siren on an ambulance, and into the white sunlight that hit me and blinded me so I blundered about and bumped into people.

It was like being back at Highford. Highford at break time. A small kid with curly hair and all these bodies pushing and shoving as you tried to keep your footing on the stairs . . .

There was suddenly a wall in front of me, so I

stopped and put a hand on it and tried to get my breath back. People were walking past me, but I shut my eyes and kept all my thoughts on breathing. And after a long time, a struggling time, someone came and leaned against the wall beside me, and it was Mum. And she stood and talked to Claire about lions and tigers and bears until I'd got my breath back, and then we walked on as if nothing had happened.

And she was stupid.

Because, as far as she was concerned, nothing had.

8

There are a million things Claire won't do; most of them are really annoying, but the good one is that she won't walk past ice-cream places.

She has a mind of her own, Stevie: she doesn't give up.

I don't eat ice cream normally — doesn't go with my image — but they had maple syrup. And by the time I'd finished letting the sun-dissolving edges of the ice cream melt on my tongue I was OK again.

It was the alarm that had got to me a bit, I think: it'd sounded a bit like a siren, and I don't like sirens — sirens and fire alarms.

But you're all right, Stevie. You were clever, and no one knew what you were trying to do.

Still, no one had realized what I'd been up to. That was the main thing. It had been a bit stupid to try to take stuff from a cabinet, though. And it had been really stupid to take Jack's word for it about the locks. It was really stupid to take Jack's word for anything when he was just a little weaselly scumbag.

Not like you, Stevie.

Jack's a total prat — he thinks he's really cool, but his mum calls him *babe* — and shoplifting's about the only thing he does know anything about. He's nicked loads of stuff — all his spray paints, for a start — and he's only been caught once or twice.

Jack was going to let me have a go with his spray paints, but I couldn't be bothered. Well, they smell really foul: we had a talk at Highford once and they said that sniffing that stuff can collapse your lungs. And those spray paints have labels all over them saying EXTREMELY FLAMMABLE and KEEP AWAY FROM SOURCES OF IGNITION, and Jack would think it was really funny to light a match to see what happened.

Anyway, there's no point in me having a go with his spray paints because I can never think of anything to write.

So do the things you can, Stevie. The things you're good at. The things anyone can do.

This shoplifting thing: well, it's just one of those

things, isn't it? I mean, practically everyone does it. Even Ben. Well, Matt doesn't, I don't think; and I don't think it's Daniel's thing, either — but then he's really rich, so he doesn't have to. And anyway, they're both really good-looking. You can *see* they're cool.

Another gift shop. The girl at the cash register was conscious, for a change, but she was talking to Claire. *Talking* to Claire? She must have been crazy — but then Claire *was* hamming up the sweet-little-girl thing for all it was worth, which couldn't have been easy wearing a witch's hat. Anyway, Mum and Claire were staging a nice distraction.

So here's your chance, Stevie.

You need a distraction when you're nicking stuff because shopkeepers are all really horrible and suspicious.

And you're brave and clever, Stevie.

Serves the shopkeepers right if they get stuff nicked, that's what I say: it's all allowed for in the price, anyway.

So do it, clever Stevie.

The electric-fizzy feeling from the devil's toenail was making my fingers itch. It was crazy, really: I mean, you don't take your *mum* shoplifting, do you? But I felt quite calm and confident — as if all I had to do was choose what I wanted.

There were these really nice steel penknives high up on a display near the back of the shop. So I put one in my pocket. And that was that. Done.

That's right, Stevie, you do as you're told. Pushover, aren't you?

I wanted to get out then, of course, but Claire was nagging Mum for some bit of rubbish — a cauldron, I think. And then two sour old ladies in flowery dresses came into the shop, and they looked at me so loathingly that my ears started growing. That happens sometimes: I don't know why. They just go red-hot all by themselves and start sprouting.

"Yes, it is nice," Mum was saying. "But it costs a lot of money, darling. Why don't we see if we can find a nicer one?"

Claire didn't scream, because she was still doing her sweet-little-ray-of-sunshine stunt; but she was beginning to scruff her feet about, and that was a danger sign.

My ears had grown to giraffe size by then, so I slouched off to bury myself in a dark corner until they deflated.

No, Stevie. Not that way. Look at the model ships or the —

And that was how it was that I noticed the other cash register, at the back of the shop. It had a beady-eyed woman sitting at it; and she was watching me.

Oh, great. Oh, tremendous.

I went really hot and my ears began to pulse like beacons. In Morse code, too: *G-U-I-L-T-Y!*

The woman at that back register *must* have seen me take the knife. There was a mirror that showed her all this side of the shop. She was just waiting until I stepped outside and then she was going to arrest me. Why hadn't I noticed her before?

I turned away from her, very carefully and slowly so my ears didn't knock down the rows of bulgy-eyed china dolls glowering down at me along the aisle, and found myself face-to-face with a security camera. Oh, *stinking* cow dung! How come I hadn't seen that?

I think someone must have been staging a distraction, Stevie.

It was pointed straight at the knife display: that *must* have caught me.

It was that electric feeling that had done it: it'd made

me feel so big, so invisible, that I hadn't even cased the joint properly. How could I have been so careless? I mean, how *could* I? Anyone would have thought I'd been *wanting* to get caught.

"Stevie! *I've* got a present!"

"Stevie, are you ready?"

Well, what's more desirable than a criminal record, Stevie?

Well, what could I do? I mean, tell me. I couldn't walk out or I'd be arrested — not that I care, obviously, the police never do anything anyway, just let you off with a caution — I think — but . . . but . . . but I couldn't put the knife back, either, now that Mum'd staggered up looking like a week-old lettuce.

Think how impressed the gang will be if you're arrested, Stevie.

So there was only one thing left for it.

Listen to me, Stevie! Listen! Let my voice be strong.

Yes. Don't laugh — *don't* laugh — but I went up and bought that stupid knife. It was really expensive, as well. It was just so *annoying*. And then I followed Mum and Claire out of the shop, clutching a pink paper bag and a nearly empty wallet.

Honestly, what a *smelly* thing to happen. And a not-like-me thing to happen, either: I mean, usually I'm quite careful.

And quite cowardly, Stevie, and quite useless; and quite amusing; and quite a challenge to make something out of you.

Anyone would have thought I was a really totally complete beginner at this sort of thing.

You see, it's us against everybody else: the gang, I mean. That's why I want to be part of it. I don't want to be like Craig Chambers, who wears a blazer and wants to be an accountant. Anyway, people pick on him a bit.

I mean, you have to look the same as everyone else, don't you — wear the same labels — but you have to be different, as well. You can be good-looking — nice trick if you can do it — or scary — and then everyone leaves you alone. I'm quite good at being scary, because I'm tall: and having such short hair helps. I have it short because if it's long it goes curly and people keep asking me why I don't clip it into the shape of a peacock.

Anyway, on the way back to the campsite — sharing the backseat with Claire and thirty-two Barbies — I discovered I was sitting on something. And it wasn't a thirty-third plastic twiglet, either. No, it wasn't. It was the devil's toenail: the all-electric, fizzier-than-warm-cola toenail that made me feel ten feet tall.

And suddenly I realized really properly what had happened in the gift shop: it was the devil's toenail that had made me feel so ten feet tall, so calm and confident, that — well, OK, I'd been a bit stupid. Not that shoplifting's stupid, obviously. Not in itself. But anyway, what that meant was — well, wow, that meant the devil's toenail was really affecting me. Wow.

How wonderful I am, Stevie. And how powerful.

But then — I went hot with excitement — power. That was what the devil's toenail was all about.

Like the gas company, Stevie: limitless power. Buy now, pay later.

I mean, now that I had the toenail, I might even end up as powerful as Daniel. Daniel's always in control of everything and everyone. Not just Ryan. No one messes with Daniel. There was this time when someone threw Daniel's sports bag into the girls' loo at school. Well, Daniel, being more or less God, just went in and got it, and the girls practically laid down a red carpet. No one knew who'd done it, but the next day Andrew Ashton had a really nasty cut on his hand, and so I think it must have been him.

That evening, when I'd finally managed to escape behind the bedspread that Mum'd pinned up to screen off my bit of the tent, I dug into my pocket and got out the devil's toenail. It was warm, and darker now that all the salt had rubbed off, and I was just so pleased with it. I balanced it on my own toe to see how it looked. Yeah. It looked a bit like a claw, and a bit like the nail of a really old person: an old person who'd dropped a hammer on his toe. And it was funny, but I really could feel the power coming off it.

Of course you can, Stevie. Because you believe in it.

I held it in my hand and closed my eyes so I could concentrate. The power was dark, like smoke — like coming out of the school gates at the end of the day when everybody's lighting up.

Yes, like smoke — like smoke that gets everywhere: into your lungs, into your blood, into your hair. Even tobacco smoke is really powerful, isn't it? It kills people all the time.

And then I thought, well, if its power was like smoke, then I could breathe it in. Get it right inside me: all through me.

So I held it in my cupped hands and I breathed deep, and as I did I thought about Daniel, and how much I wanted to have his sort of power.

And the fizzing of the devil's toenail went through

me — up my arms, and through me — until I could feel it deep inside me. Deep, deep inside. And for a while I could feel it; but then I stopped noticing it, but it was there all the same.

It was inside me. Its power was mine, and I was a new person. It was part of me.

Part of me, Stevie. You're part of me.

Suddenly, just for a moment, I seemed to hear faraway triumphant laughter.

No smoke without fire.

I must have fallen asleep holding it.

I dreamt about sharp-voiced crowds that laughed plumes of flame.

10

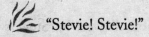 "Stevie! Stevie!"

Someone had got me and I couldn't get free. I did everything I could, but I was falling, falling, through biting flames, with strong hands clutching me.

"Stevie!"

The ground came up at me, but somehow I missed it and plunged into something soft — and suddenly it was daytime and the walls were the wrong color. And Mum was holding on to me.

I rolled away from her, tipped off my air mattress, and ended up with my face buried in my sleeping bag.

"Are you all right?"

The only way to make her go away was to answer.

So I sort of grunted.

She stood up straight.

"I'm sorry to come in, Stevie, but you were having a bad dream."

I lay there and didn't say anything. It was none of her business, anyway.

Then Claire's voice piped up.

"You were screaming," she said, primly. "*I* don't scream like that, do I, Mummy?"

Mum turned on her.

"Claire, you know you're not allowed in Stevie's bedroom."

"It isn't a bedroom: it's just one side of the tent with a bedspread hanging down. Anyway, I don't, do I, Mummy?"

"Not when you're asleep, no," said Mum. "I just wish it were the same when you're awake. Now, come on, and we'll leave Stevie to finish waking up."

OK, so I scream in my sleep sometimes. It doesn't happen so much now. It's just one of those things. It's a bit embarrassing when I'm in the tent, though. And it means I can't go and sleep over at people's houses. Matt asked me once, but I said I was going mountain climbing — which was a bit silly, really, because there isn't a mountain within a hundred miles of my house. But Matt didn't say anything.

Anyway, having a whole procession of people

rampaging about in my room had put an end to my sleeping in, so I got up.

Dad was missing, but none of us was surprised. He always sneaks off bird-watching if he wakes up first.

"Honestly," said Mum. "We're only here for two days. You'd think he could hang around that long."

"He's mean and selfish," said Claire, cheerfully, "and I'm going to use my new cauldron to cast an evil spell on him."

"Good girl," said Mum, vaguely, and poured herself some coffee.

So there we were stuck at the site, waiting for Dad. We couldn't go anywhere, because of course the site was situated in pleasant countryside miles from anywhere except more pleasant countryside.

I went and sat on my air mattress and had nothing to do. It wasn't fair.

Claire began chanting her evil spell. She was doing it in this really stupid voice, like a constipated goat's, and it was just so annoying. And it's difficult to feel ten feet tall when you're in a tent that only just clears six feet, even when you've got a devil's toenail in your hands.

They all treat you so badly, Stevie. It isn't fair.

And suddenly I felt really angry: and it was unusual

for me to feel angry with Dad, because on the whole I was used to him.

And then a thought came to me from somewhere: and I thought, *magic spell*?

So I rubbed my thumb over the devil's toenail until I felt the fizzing power working its way up my fingers.

That's right, Stevie. Just do as I tell you.

And then, I did things.

I went into the loo and pulled a hair off Dad's comb.

Then I slipped back behind the bedspread that screened off my side of the tent.

And I began to use my power.

11

I put the devil's toenail on the ground cloth. Then I knelt in front of it and curled the hair round it into a circle.

That looked classy, sort of magical — not that I believe in magic, obviously, haven't for ages, not ever, really: not ordinary sorts of magic, anyway. But this was something different. Something special.

Right. Now I had power. Lots and lots of power.

And somehow it was as if a small voice inside me was whispering: *Think revenge.*

The power was like a bud: quite suddenly it opened up all round me, so big that things went out of focus and made me dizzy. And the small voice inside me was saying, *You can have whatever you want*: and it was showing me pictures of all the different things I could do.

It was so confusing that I almost wished for the wrong thing. I mean, it was all very well to think, *Make Dad fall off a cliff;* but then how would we get home?

(Mum doesn't drive: she's useless.) And when I thought about Dad falling — his coat going up over his head, and his legs kicking — well, I sort of decided it wouldn't be practical.

But parents are the enemy, Stevie. You don't care about them.

I was so dizzy by then that I wasn't even sure which way up I was; but at the same time I felt like you do when you're at the top of a really big slide — and I knew I had to let myself go for anything to happen. Just for a moment I almost chickened out; but the something inside me was still whispering about revenge, and of course it was right. Well, when you have enemies you have to get your own back, don't you? If you don't, they just do more and more and make fun of you for being useless. At my old school there was a boy like that and things got worse and worse for him.

So what would a cool person do, Stevie?

When you look at the cool people, they've all got the right idea, which is to hit back really hard. Gavin Osbourne, he said Daniel was gay, and Daniel and Jack were going to break his arm; but Gavin said sorry and kissed Daniel's feet just before the joint cracked. Matt said it was just messing about.

But this is real, Stevie. Real. Real. Real.

The devil's toenail fizzed suddenly, fiercely, and somehow everything around scooped itself up and wrapped itself round me: and suddenly I was either somewhere dark, or else my eyes had stopped working. And that was such a surprise that I think I must have lost concentration for a moment; at any rate, my fingers had opened and the devil's toenail was falling down onto the ground.

Stevie! Listen to me, and I will give you —

But then there was a voice. It cut through the darkness like acid; and as soon as that happened I was back in the real world — I almost heard a *click!* — and I could see again, and it was Mum. And she was saying something about toast. So I put the devil's toenail in my pocket and went and had some.

I wasn't really sure what had happened. I mean, I hadn't really *thought* anything much — I hadn't even got round to deciding what I wanted to happen to Dad. But the power of the devil's toenail: well, it was really really strong. Quite scary, in a way. Not that I was scared, obviously.

But anyway, I was back in the real world where only ordinary things happened. And in the ordinary world there was Claire, who made me play with her — well, she kept hitting me with her wand; and I think I was still a bit too weak from — whatever it was that'd happened — to resist. We've got this game where we get all Claire's Barbies and tie blindfolds round their heads, and then we line them up against a wall and shoot them with elastic bands.

Yeah, I know, but it keeps her quiet.

So I'd forgotten all about everything except firing squads until Mum finally stopped fidgeting about the dirty dishes/dirty clothes/breakfast stuff and said, *"Dad's late!"*

And I had this feeling as if I was a drainpipe and there was cold water running all the way down inside me.

12

By the end of half an hour Mum had rambled her way through all the likely things — watch stopped, traffic jam, lost — and after an hour she started on the nasties: car accident, falling down a cliff, murder.

And then of course Claire made things even worse.

"I bet he *is* dead," she said calmly.

No one said anything.

"So can I have his binoculars?"

You have to be really really patient with Claire, but just for a moment Mum forgot.

"Don't talk nonsense!" she said, exasperated. She went into the loo and shut the door, and I seized my chance to escape to my space behind the bedspread. A car turned into our drive, but I knew it wasn't ours even before I looked. Our car sounds like a rock-powered sewing machine.

What if he *didn't* come back? Well, I mean, it

wouldn't be *my* fault — there wouldn't be anything you could prove, not in a court of law.

What if he didn't come back?

Another car. I was sure it wasn't, but of course I looked anyway. I heard Mum open a window so she could look, too. The car was the right color, and —

And no. It was going past.

Of course he wasn't dead. He was always late. He *liked* being late. And I hadn't really wanted anything much to happen.

The devil's toenail was warm in my pocket.

I'll throw it away, I thought, suddenly. Throw it back in the sea.

It's too late for that, Stevie. You're on the downward slope, now. Can't you feel yourself sliding?

Oh God, I thought, I didn't mean it. Not really. Look, if you'll just make it all right then I'll —

"Mummy! There he is!"

Mum and I bumped into each other going out to look. It looked — yes, it was. It was Dad.

You know, if he'd been ten seconds later I might have made some really serious promises: but then I suppose it wouldn't have made any difference, because I'd only have broken them.

Dad was pink with sweat and bother and he seemed even flabbier than usual. He said he was sorry he was late, and Mum said not to worry. She always says that. Sometimes she means it, and sometimes she snaps at him all afternoon to serve him right.

"Much traffic?" asked Mum, which meant *you'd better have a good excuse.*

And he did.

He sat down, heaved up a shuddering, tragic, put-upon sigh, whined fretfully about the heat, said he was sure he'd got sunstroke — and told us he'd been arrested.

"What?"

And he had. Really. My dad, in trouble with the police. I mean, it was quite cool. It was really funny, too, because he'd been arrested for trying to steal a car. He'd been seen trying all the doors, you see. They'd arrested him and he'd had to sit in the police car while they were very nice to him. And he'd explained that the reason that he'd been trying all the doors was that it was his own car, and that he'd just gone back to check he'd locked it.

How we laughed.

"It's your own fault for not shaving," said Mum,

unsympathetically. "You *look* like a villain. All you need is LOOT written on your bag and you'd be all complete."

"You'd have to be mad to steal our car," I pointed out. "It's all rusty. And full of mud. And it smells of Claire's puke."

"It's not fair," said Claire. "I wish they'd sent you to prison. I'd *like* to visit a prison."

Anyway, Claire could hardly wait to get back and tell all her friends, and Mum could hardly wait to get back and tell the neighbors, and I — Well, it probably wasn't cool to talk about Dad to the gang. But it was still funny. It was so funny that I dug my hand into my pocket and sort of said thanks. You know, to the devil's toenail.

But I could have done so much more, Stevie: things beyond your nightmares.

Next time we must make sure you aren't distracted by the enemy, mustn't we?

13

OK. It was Bank Holiday Monday and the last day of our lovely holiday. Now, holidays: well, let's go through the gang, shall we? Daniel, he goes on karting holidays to far-flung five-star continents; Matt goes to a classy resort in Spain with fifteen pools and a built-in snob factor; Jack goes to Ibiza; Ryan goes to his auntie's in Scarborough; even *Ben* goes to stay on his dad's houseboat.

And what do I do?

Yes, I get to spend the afternoon waiting outside a garage.

That's right: the police had said one of Dad's tires was thin, so our outing for the last day of the holiday was a long irritable halt-and-lurch drive to find a garage that opened on a Bank Holiday so we could get a new one.

Brilliant.

I sat on the wall outside watching the traffic — the smell of petrol makes me puke, so I don't go in those places — and the sun was bouncing off all the rows and rows of super-shiny showroom cars straight into my eyes. Loads of cars, there were, all with their doors open, like cormorants holding out their stiff wings to the sun.

I sat with my hands in my pockets watching the traffic going past. All the cars were really new and shiny. Well, compared with ours they were, anyway. Why didn't Dad get a car that wasn't made of recycled baked-bean tins and sun-paled plastic?

You should have got rid of him while you had the chance, Stevie.

A little girl pointed at me as she swept past in her car, so I hopped over the wall out of sight.

There were so many cars, all lined up in rows.

Look, Stevie. Look at that one.

There was a red Mercedes right by the exit. Its leather seats were veined with expensive creases.

There was no one about. And why shouldn't I have a sit in it? I had to adjust the driver's seat because it was too far forward.

The steering wheel was warm; warm like a basking lion.

Comfortable, isn't it, Stevie?

Yes, this was where I should be.

Everything was easy. Easy.

So start the car, Stevie.

And Jack said you could start any car with a penknife.

You'd really have style, then. You'd be who you should be.

Yeah, I'd drive really fast — skid the car round corners on two tires. That'd impress the gang. Even Daniel only drove off-road.

The ignition was on the steering column.

Steering column: yes, I knew all the words.

And . . . and there was the keyhole.

There. Waiting. A bright ring, and a jagged hole.

Waiting. Waiting.

I'd have to turn on the ignition with my penknife, depress the clutch, put the car in gear, press the accelerator, take off the handbrake, turn the wheel.

How did I know all those things? How did I know?

Never mind that.

It's easy, Stevie. Now — fly.

I'd go so fast it would be like flying. That's the thing I want to do most in all the world.

So.

Start the car, Stevie.

Starting the car will make a noise.

There's no one to hear, Stevie. Start it!

And what if I don't steer it right and it goes into the wall?

So what? It's not yours, Stevie. Start it!

I —

Start it, Stevie. Start it. Start it.

And the knife slides neatly into the keyhole. Goes in cleanly, easily, like a cat through a gate. And then —

That car was so beautiful it almost brought tears to my eyes. Dad's car sounded like a brick-filled tumble dryer: this one just went *churrrrrrrrrrrrr*. I had a panicky moment when I turned the wheel too far — I wasn't expecting the power-steering — and I nearly stalled it; but I managed to straighten it up and then suddenly I was bumping down the curb and onto the road. I went softly and slowly past the office, full as it was of old wobbly idiot-people; but then my car was away and free and just one with the others. I eased down on the accelerator. Yeah: I could do it. I could do it, and I loved it.

Then the engine was roaring. Power. That car had so much power.

Power not doing very much.

Change gear. I needed to change gear.

But that's tricky.

Never mind. I've got this far and —

There. There. Hardly a crunch, and the car stretches forward like a well-oiled cheetah. And this is the best thing ever, because the road is wide and empty and suddenly I can do it. So I put my foot down to the boards — switch gears, and switch gears again — and then the engine breathes freely. And because there's no one about I press a button on the dashboard and something goes *chunk* very softly and then with a confident hum the hood folds back on itself so that the wind ruffles my shirt and I have to put my shades on.

I'm on the coast road now, and leaning back and steering with one hand as it skirts the cliffs. And I'm not scared at all, even though it's all bleached outcrops of rock and hairpin bends. But then I catch a glimpse of something behind me in my mirror, and it's a blue light, and half a second later a strident siren bursts the calm, and my heart lurches with excitement. I put my foot down hard. It's dangerous, now, but I have to take risks if I'm going to escape, and anyway I love taking risks, it's my lifeblood. I throw the car at a bend, but I'm not prepared for the second turn, and the back of the car slews round through the dust right to the edge of the cliff and I lose pace waiting for the tires to spin themselves to a grip.

The only thing that saves me is that the car behind doesn't make the bend. The first sign I have is a blue light reflecting off the rocks in an odd place; and then there's a crash, and I don't know what's happened. But there's no time to worry.

The sea is vivid blue and the sand has blown a pale gauze across the road. The car is full of power and it's all mine. I can outrun anything.

Everything is perfect; but then I pass a house by the side of the road, and then another, and I find myself heading into town. That's a bit tricky, because here there are lots of junctions and traffic lights. But I'm confident now, and my beautiful red car, as long as a spaceship, makes everyone look. There are two girls in bikinis who shade their eyes and smile: and I would stop, of course, except that I've already got a gorgeous girlfriend who's a model, which is quite surprising, because although she's really stunning she's not that thin.

And then I start to recognize things: a shop, a pub, a church, a traffic light.

I suppose it's not too early for them to put in their summer plants down here, said Mum, long ago.

I turn one last corner. I'm nearly out of fuel, now, so I have to stop. I reverse the car stylishly into its space between two others, pull on the brake, and get out.

With absolutely perfect timing.

"Ah, there you are," said Dad. "We're all done."

And so we drove back to the camper, and I was really happy because I could tell the gang all about it and they'd know I was really cool.

THE END

14

What good are you to me, Stevie? What good are you to anyone?

All right. All *right*. It was true up to me starting the car up. Well, the penknife wouldn't turn the ignition on, would it?

What does it matter whether it's true or not, anyway? What *does* it matter?

It matters because no one else will believe it either.

What good are you to anyone, Stevie?

I got Dad to drop me off by the pool and I went down to the beach. The beach where I'd found the devil's toenail. I still had it in my pocket. All that power, and I still wasn't any good to anyone.

Yes. Look at yourself, Stevie.

I was the only one on the beach who was alone, do you know that? Even the old ones with Panama hats and bunions were waddling along in couples. And I felt . . . I felt as if someone was disemboweling me with that penknife.

And you don't even know how to steal a car, Stevie.

(A penknife to steal a car? I don't know who was the more pathetic, Jack for saying it or me for believing it.)

No wonder you're on your own. Who'd want to be with you, Stevie? Because you're useless.

Whenever you meet people — you know, when you're with your parents — they always say two things: *haven't you grown?* and *have you got a girlfriend?* God, they are all so cruel.

It's not that I really *want* a girlfriend — I mean, I'm not desperate. I can't see the point, really. I mean, girls are horrible. They sit and look at you for ages, pityingly, and then in the end they ask you what conditioner you use. I'm not even sure what conditioner's *for* — and anyway, I haven't got enough hair to bother now. *Shampoo's* practically a waste of time for me.

Don't think I'm gay, though, because I'm not. I'm sure I'm not. I mean, the thought of sitting on Ryan, like Daniel does, turns my stomach. And when I'm in the corridor I always try to plan it so I get to push my way past the girls.

Not that Daniel's gay, no way: he's got this magnetic force, and any girl who comes anywhere near him gets drawn in. Girls like Matt, too, but Daniel's really sort of charming, that's the thing they go for. The shiny manners. At school he goes around in a heap of girls all showing off their legs and pushing lipsticky grins at him. Horrible. They'd do anything for him: they're as bad as Ryan. You know, I can see why the girls are all over Daniel, but I don't know why Ryan is, really, because Daniel keeps telling Ryan he's got smelly armpits and dog breath and needs industrial-strength deodorant; but Ryan thinks it's hilarious and does silly dances so Daniel can see his fat wobble.

But Daniel and Ryan have friends, don't they, Stevie? You can't even manage that. What is the point of you?

I climbed up onto the sewage pipe that ran out rustily across the beach and far out to sea. And I thought, if I walked along that and jumped off the end, then I might drown: me, and the devil's toenail with me.

That's right, Stevie. You're no good to me. Why clutter up the world?

And in a way I wanted to do it; but then I thought about it properly: the struggling for breath, the swallowing the salty sewage; and I was too much of a coward.

No wonder people hate you, Stevie. Don't you wish you could just go to sleep and never wake up?

Pills would be better. Yes, if I could just get hold of some sleeping pills. Mum would be upset, but she'd know why I'd done it. I might even get into the paper:

BULLIED BOY COMMITS SUICIDE.

There.

There.

There.

OK?

Now you know. And I hope you're satisfied.

That's why I left my old school, because I got picked on. I tried to stick it out, but I couldn't, and so I had to leave.

But I haven't been bullied at this school.

No way.

So you're damaged goods, Stevie. All right. Now I know, it's something to build on, isn't it?

Fear. Hatred.

Delicious. So. Listen to me, Stevie: listen to me, and I'll make you someone worthwhile.

I've learned a lot since I was at Highford.

Me and the devil's toenail.

15

Believe it or not, when I got back Mum and Dad were watching a car chase.

Yes, on the telly. How else?

"I'd like to do that," said Claire, as the first car went up a ramp, turned through the air in slow motion, landed, and then zoomed off the wrong way along a tram track.

"When you're older," said Dad, absently.

The car on the telly went through a pool of oil, skidded, and blew up. The whole screen swirled with churning smoke and spiky flame.

Fire. Fire, *no* —

Have courage, Stevie!

Mum switched the channel.

"I was watching that!" said Claire.

So Mum gave her the remote control, but by the time Claire had worked out which way up it went, it had switched to a shot of two scowling American policemen striding down a corridor.

Claire kicked out at the table leg and nearly collapsed the whole thing. Everything in the camper was made so it folded: it was like living in an origami doll's house.

"I want to drive *now*," she said.

"Daniel's got his own kart," I said. "It's really expensive. He took it up this steep bank in his garden and cut down a whole load of wildflowers. His dad went berserk."

Mum sniffed the way she always did when Daniel was mentioned. She didn't like Daniel because he'd done so many brilliant things: she was afraid I'd copy him and then she'd lose her power over me.

I don't know what Daniel's mum's like, but she must be really cool. I mean, she let Daniel go to boarding school. It sounded incredible. There was this boy at Daniel's old school, and he sniffed some deodorant from an aerosol can and it killed him. He was in the cricket pavilion — it was a really posh school — and he rushed out and collapsed. One of the teachers tried to give him the kiss of life, but he was dead on arrival. It was in the paper and everything. Matt asked Daniel about it, but Daniel's so cool he just said it happened just before he left, and that the boy was a prat and it had served him right.

"If I could drive then Mummy wouldn't have to take me swimming," said Claire. "*Or* to Brownies. And I could take Katie, too."

Mum smiled and kissed Claire's hair.

"I'm not sure she'd be brave enough to drive with you," she said.

"Oh, yes, she would. She'd like it. Katie likes screaming."

And suddenly I found myself wishing that I had a friend like that. Just someone ordinary, to enjoy things with. They wouldn't have to be cool or anything. Just someone I could be free with: if I had a friend like that then I wouldn't even need the power of the devil's toenail because . . . because I'd know that when I was with him I'd be safe.

Just for a moment I wished Matt wasn't in the gang.

No you don't, Stevie.

But no, I didn't really, because —

Because the gang's cool, Stevie. And so it's the right place for you to be.

The thing is that being in the gang's really cool. I

mean, they do graffiti and nicking stuff and really good stuff like that.

And you're learning how to be cool, too, Stevie.

And I was learning how to be cool, too.

So your life will glow with power, Stevie.

So everything was rosy. Everything was cool.

16

We had a scrappy un-matching leftovers meal, and packed up. I had to help Dad take down the tent and hitch up the camper, Mum spent an hour making sure the camper was surgically clean, and Claire whacked her air mattress flat with her wand and got underfoot generally.

Then it was driving back home, slowly, jerkily, through the exhausted Bank Holiday traffic.

Are we nearly there yet?

On, and on, and on, and on to the highway, and past signs to Reading, and signs to Reading, and signs to Reading, miles and miles.

"That was Grandma's turn off," I said, just slightly too late.

"That's right."

"But what about the camper?"

"Oh, we're keeping it. Then we can go away next weekend as well."

"What??"

"It's a pity we couldn't have stayed for the whole week, really, but Dad couldn't get the holiday."

And of course Dad kept driving no matter what I said — *it's not fair, you never told me, my opinion doesn't count for anything in this family, I can't wait to leave home* — but he drove on and on, and then on to another highway, and under the jets of Heathrow, and on, and on, until my mind was numb with the monotony of it and I could have been anywhere.

And then suddenly we'd fallen off the highway and we were back in the real world. And everything was green, green and lush. It was only home, I know, but . . . but it looked like a different place.

But it was the same. All the people were the same. Everything was the same.

Except me.

Because now I had the devil's toenail. And I was getting stronger: I could feel its power inside me, spreading like ink through blotting paper.

And soon, Stevie, you are going to do whatever I say.

So soon I'd be able to do anything. Anything I wanted.

That's pride, Stevie.

Good start.

17

 Home.

I got up so early there was still dew on the grass. It was absolutely quiet — the waiting stillness you get before everyone wakes up and spoils it. Just think, all those thousands and millions of years, and every day spoiled. Brilliant, isn't it?

The early morning's the best time to be out if you want to be alone. Everything clear and quiet except for the flop and squeak of your shoes on the silver grass.

I had the devil's toenail in my pocket and we were looking for things to smash.

I know some people don't see the point of smashing things: they're happy as they are. Ryan's like that, even though he's always the last one to be picked for games, even after me. That's why Daniel likes him so much. Daniel can sit on him, play the slave game, call him anything — *fatball, smell-bomb, mutant* — and Ryan just laughs and laughs until his asthma makes him wheeze and his eyes disappear into little pouches of fat.

It was funny, because once Matt said to Daniel, *One day someone's going to kill you.* I think it was a joke, because no one would dare. Anyway, Daniel's really really cool, so why should anyone want to?

Farmstate School's got railings all the way round to keep all the violent crazed lunatics in; but the gate's always wide open, and at seven o'clock on the Tuesday of half-term break, the place echoed with cheap emptiness. The swimming pool had been filled and covered in a layer of bubble wrap. That'd be easy. I had my knife. I could slash the whole cover to shreds and they'd have to close the pool. I imagined it: the pool filled with a sludge of strips of plastic, the filter blocked, and a pale pudgy caretaker in shirtsleeves and corduroy trousers scratching his head at the damage.

Plunging your knife in, Stevie: plunging it in right to the hilt.

Ripping. Destroying. Making it *my* world.

Get out your knife, Stevie.

It was a beautiful knife. The steel of the handle drew in the heat of the sun and the blade gleamed like a claw.

Made for ripping, Stevie.

Made for ripping, my knife was: but the plastic was tough, and the water underneath made it shift massively like a basking whale when I tried. The first blow was useless — it skidded off into nothing more than an ice rink scar and a wispy shaving. So I struck again, hard, and the plastic heaved with the water like skin on a flabby body: but then the blade caught, and entered, and punctured the plastic; and as it did it was as if a little bit of myself escaped.

So I did it again. And again; and each time a bit of myself that had been inside me under pressure came away; and as the pressure went I began to shrink and harden into a different shape.

That's it, Stevie: let all the useless bits of yourself go.

I changed my grip so I could stab down harder. Stab down. Stab *down*. And I was ten feet tall again; and strong, strong, like stone. And stabbing, and stabbing; and now I had the skill I could rip the stuff, too. Rip it to shreds.

I carried on until all the bits of me that could escape had gone. I was tired by then. I'd forgotten all about the outside world — but when I looked around everything was still empty and quiet; and all that had changed was that the silver had vanished from the grass.

Another blazing day.

And look at what you've done, Stevie.

The pool was covered in a smooth roll of shimmering plastic — except in one corner. There it was slashed and ripped and ugly.

And wasn't it wonderful? Wasn't it part of the new-improved Stevie-style universe? Well, of course it was. Of course it was. It was just like Jack would have done.

Oh, yes. Oh, yes, it was wonderful. *I* was wonderful. I'd established my power over bits of plastic throughout the world, hadn't I? I mean, I'd really sorted out that bit of bubble wrap. I mean, *wow*.

Wasn't I brilliant? Wasn't I? Wasn't it just the sort of thing Daniel would have done?

Never. Never in a million years. Never. Never.

It wasn't cool enough, wasn't clever enough, wasn't powerful enough: didn't come close.

So you're good at hatred, Stevie. That's good, it's powerful stuff. But don't fritter it all away on yourself. Turn it on other people, where it can be useful.

Daniel says — he knows ever such a lot, does Daniel — *Power corrupts and absolute power corrupts absolutely.* You only have to look around you to see how true it is. I mean, teachers.

There was this teacher at my old school. He was

called Mitchell, and he just fancied himself so much. He was one of the ones who used to dress up as a professor: you know, tweed jacket, half-glasses.

God, I hated him. I can feel it now, remembering. He was always getting at me, and it wasn't because I was ugly or stupid or nasty or irritating, it was because he was frightened of the others. I used to hang around in the corridor so I went in just before Mitchell did — it was safer — and one time the class had been having this fight and one of the chairs had got smashed up. So all the girls were in one corner out of the way, and the usual three boys wearing square glasses were talking about quantum theory in another. And I walked in. And then Mitchell walked in behind me and said, *What's all this?* And of course Gary Towers said, *It was Stephen Saunders, sir. He went berserk.* And, of course, of course, of *course*, Mitchell (who'd just seen me walk into the classroom, remember?) gave me a double detention.

And everybody knew it was just because he was frightened of Gary Towers. Oh, damn.

I'm really glad I'm out of that one.

Be really glad you're no longer that person, Stevie. Be glad that fool is dead. And be careful to keep him that way.

I'm here to help you.

18

No one stays the same forever. It isn't possible. You change as the world changes. It's evolution, really, I suppose: evolution or extinction.

When I was in nursery school they used to say, *Hands together and eyes closed*, and then Mr. Johnson would say, *Our Father in Heaven . . .* The naughty boys used to nudge each other and giggle, and sometimes it felt as if you were the only one in the whole school who really had your eyes closed. But Mr. Johnson was really nice, and he knew all sorts of stuff, and once when someone kicked me in the playground he told them off and they had to say sorry and stand in the corridor at playtime. And all the time they all used to say, *Love one another*, until in the end you sort of got used to it. It didn't do any good, obviously; but at least everyone was agreed on the principle.

And then I went to Highford and suddenly I was an outcast.

It was having curly hair that did it.

I still don't really understand why it's so bad to have curly hair. Just don't understand it. The first day, I went home and Mum said, *Did you have a nice time?* and all I wanted to do was go away and cry. I remember standing in the hall, trying to get my tie off: but I couldn't remember which bit to pull, and it was like being a slave wearing a ball and chain. And then I told Mum it was all right and went and had my cry in the loo.

You know, I've only just realized, but Claire's hair would be curly if she didn't always have plaits. And Dad's is, but then it probably didn't matter in the olden days. And — hang on — Simon Fallan's was, too — why didn't I think of that before? — because no one used to get on at him. He was actually one of the cool ones. He used to carry a comb in the pocket of his blazer and comb his hair before every lesson. And smirk a lot.

They used to get at me all the time. All the time. There was a whole group of them, and that was what they did for fun. There was this time in Science. Someone got a bottle of nitric acid and burned holes in some books. I don't know exactly who did it, but of course I've got a good idea. Anyway, they said it was me.

What I'd do now, of course, is swear blind that I

hadn't. But — I don't know — in storybooks they used to say, *Don't tell tales,* and I sort of thought (well, I was only in Year Seven) that they might lay off me if I took the blame.

But it just made them think I was stupid and mad, as well as posh. Posh, that was the killer. Only posh people bother with all that moral stuff, you see. But I'm not posh. Mind you, they knew that all right because Mum had got me the wrong shoes for PE. So they used to say I was squalid — they enjoyed that word, *squalid* — and they said I lived in a cardboard box. But now, of course, I understand.

It was obvious, really. They weren't making fun of me because I had curly hair. They were making fun of me because I was me.

19

I had to look after Claire in the afternoon while Mum went in to work. Claire's got a million sticky little friends, but they don't come round all that much. Mum did phone round to try to get rid of her, but loads of people were away for half term, and the rest were at the dentist.

"Try to be patient with her, Stevie," said Mum, as she winced her way into her work shoes. "Claire," she went on, without hope, "try to be a good girl, darling."

So there I was, in charge.

What do you want to do to her, Stevie?

But the thing about Claire is that she's a six-year-old little girl with pigtails and a face like a plucked owl's. I mean, she's revolting: I didn't want *anything* to do with her.

It was all right to start with, because she took herself out into the garden and pulled up flowers to make a spell for her cauldron. But then she wanted me to dance round the garden with her chanting the incredibly magic words:

Abracadabra, kazam kazoo,

Wobbling willies and kangaroo poo . . .

and when I wouldn't she got angry, and she kept trying to push me out of the front door so she could lock me out. She's a vicious little cat, but she's really small and weedy, so it was quite funny, really. So then she started screaming, *You're ugly, I hate you*. But still I didn't do anything to her, except just enough to stop her locking me out, even when she started kicking me. Well, I did laugh a bit. But then she got really riled and she lashed out with her wand and got me right on the point of the elbow. Well, I mean, that *hurts*.

Quick, Stevie! Get her!

But it was like trying to catch a weasel with your bare hands: she was all quicksilver dodging and tight turns and in the end it turned out she'd got big enough to reach the bolt on the bathroom door.

Mum got home to find that Claire had emptied a bottle of shampoo all over the floor and put the toilet roll down the loo.

And of course it was all my fault. And after I'd stayed in to look after the smelly little rat as well.

"It was only one afternoon," said Mum, after I'd finished telling her how totally unfair she was. "You've still got all evening, if you want to go out."

So then, of course, I had to.

20

That evening, when it was getting dark, I took my bike out. I rode up to the hills and through the grayness towards the quarry. Just me and the devil's toenail. I hadn't told the gang I was back from holiday, so I didn't have to go to the park. And I wanted to get away from everything.

No chance of that, Stevie. I'm here with you for good.
Well, not exactly for good.

But it doesn't work like that: sometimes it's hard not to take things with you. Round and round. That's how it used to be all the time when I was at Highford, but it's mostly all right now.

There is one good thing about school, though.

Yes, there is, really.

It's that you leave.

Yes!

So school gets better all the time because leaving is nearer. More real. Once you're out of Year Seven and you see all the minuscule little new kids tiptoeing around carrying their maps upside down, then you realize how far you've come. But so has everyone else, of course.

Yes — the others have got more inventive.

There was a wind blowing up on the hills and all around were really heavy big churning clouds: and there was this little path that went right along the edge of the quarry, and sometimes it went so near you could look down, down, down, over crumbled pillars of mildewed chalk, right to the bottom. And the sun was shining, which was strange, because there was only ever one little gap in the clouds — but for the whole of that evening the sun shone. And it was beautiful, and I knew it was beautiful; but somehow all the beauty stayed outside me and I couldn't feel it.

When I was at Highford — I kept trying to push the thoughts away, but they kept falling back — so. When I was at Highford.

It's all in the past now, anyway. In the *past*.

When I was at Highford I used to wish I was dead. Really wish it.

What do you want for your birthday, Stevie?

To be dead, I'd want to say; but of course I wouldn't. I didn't tell Mum or Dad about it. Still haven't. Won't ever. It's not the telling tales, or worrying that I'll get beaten up. No, it's not that. I don't care about any of the people at Highford anymore.

That's true, you know.

I hadn't realized that before. Not that it makes any difference, because people are the same everywhere. That's the thing.

Anyway. The reason I never told Mum and Dad about being picked on was the humiliation. Because, you see, Mum and Dad think I'm all right. The way parents do. And Mum would have been really upset and angry. And she would have wanted to go up to the school, and that would only have made things worse. Because everything made things worse.

You know, there's nothing you can do. *Turn the other cheek,* they say. And what happens?

Well, guess.

Not difficult, is it?

There are these geese in the park in town, and there are always one or two that are bleeding and raw because they've had their wings pecked out by the others. You can see it happening sometimes. Attack, attack, and there's no hiding place. And sometimes I look at those geese, with just a few quills poking crookedly out of their sides and their feathers stained with blood, and I try to work out, *why them?* But I don't get it. I suppose their legs are the wrong shade of orange, or their feathers lie the wrong way, or they've got a funny way of honking, or they're scared of water.

I've seen them try to fight back — but then loads of the others weigh in and it's worse than ever.

And everybody walks by because it isn't their business.

But why shouldn't they, Stevie? What good would it be to them?

The thing is that nice doesn't *win*. That's all there is to it. And really, as Dad says (but about other things, of course), if you can't beat them, join them.

That's right. Start again, Stevie. Be a new person.

Going to a different school was a good idea. It was a new start, you see, and I'd learned things. And I had short hair: and every time I looked at someone, I thought about hitting them.

That really works, that does: even scares the teachers.

Right. So I'd got that sorted out.

The next thing was to get some support: because even if you're James Bond you still get done over by the wimp in the gang. See? Simple.

I didn't know why I hadn't worked that out before. I

mean, even *Ryan* had that one worked out, and he's barely got the brains of a retarded peanut. He'd got himself into the gang without any looks or talents; all he was good at was not caring when people insulted him — that, and doing as he was told.

Daniel just loved him. Ryan was his own personal slave, you see, that he could experiment on. Daniel had it all worked out.

There was this time Daniel told Ryan that if you cut a cat's tail off it didn't hurt it, but you just turned it into a Manx, which was really valuable. And Jack got this cat and Ryan would have done it, only Matt laughed so much that everyone couldn't help joining in and the cat got away. And then everybody said Ryan was a moron; but I was sort of glad, because cats can be really vicious and Ryan wouldn't have been the same with big scars all over him. Ryan's more the fat baby type.

If only I was like Daniel, then everything would be all right. I'd be in charge, then, you see, and people wouldn't be able to . . . to do anything I didn't want them to. Perhaps now that I had the devil's toenail —

What do you want, Stevie? What do you really want, then? Deep down in the darkness inside you?

All right. What did I want to happen?

I got the devil's toenail out of my pocket, and I closed my eyes and rubbed the devil's toenail, and I said: *Make Daniel go away, make Daniel go away, make Daniel go away.* And the devil's toenail fizzed under my fingers and I felt myself change inside, as I did when it did things.

Make Daniel go away? Don't you dare even to wish him dead, Stevie? And I thought you were learning to hate. And what a bargain that would be. You, instead of Daniel.

I'm tired of you, Stevie.

And — I'm not exactly sure where the thought came from — but I suddenly realized that the only way to get Daniel out of my way was to ride my bike over the edge of the quarry.

And all your troubles will be over, Stevie.

And I was going to do it.

And then you'll be with me forever and ever, Stevie.

I was.

I sat there on the edge and looked down and down to the bottom of the quarry, far, far away.

Go on, Stevie. Do something cool for once.

But — I was too scared.

How can you live, Stevie? When you're worse than nothing.

Too scared to be by myself, and too scared to earn my way into the gang, and too scared to jump.

No way out. No way out. No way out.

I rode back home. The sun was low and the grass swayed bronze.

Don't think you've got a chance, Stevie. I'll get you, soon: to live for me or die for me, it's all the same. My voice is getting stronger, isn't it? Stronger, inside you. You won't be able to fight it much longer.

And I felt like a piece of a jigsaw that had got into the wrong box.

21

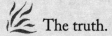 The truth.

OK.

Ready?

I went for a walk one night — when I was still at Highford, there's nothing much to it really — and some people from school had some petrol. And they threw it over me and set me alight.

There. Simple. That's all it was. I'm quite better now, thank you. Except for the scarring, obviously: that, and not having any hair on the left-hand side. But my ear has been rebuilt and you'd hardly know, except for the fact that it looks as if it's made out of red rubber. And I have to have my hair very short, obviously, or I'd look moth-eaten.

There you are.

So what?

Yes, it did hurt. And yes, I was in the hospital for a long time. A long time.

At this point someone usually says I was lucky not to lose my sight; and what I want to say — only I never do, somehow, because they're always sad, old people — is, *Yes, and you're lucky not to have been set on fire, aren't you?*

But do you know what the worst thing is? The worst thing — the very very worst thing — is that I'm frightened. All the time, nearly. I can carry on, mostly, but it's there, at the back of my mind. I suppose I'm getting used to it, because I don't worry too much about going to sleep now. And there was one time I didn't have a bad dream for four days: but it didn't last.

It makes me angry. Really, really angry.

When I was little we used to have a barbecue in the back garden sometimes, and it was the best thing ever. We used to build the stand out of bricks and I used to help Dad cook burgers. I loved it.

But now we don't have them anymore. Mum and Dad don't suggest it. We pretend barbecues don't exist: but we all know it's because I'd throw up. It's the smell of scorching flesh, mostly, I think. That's why I'm angry, you see: it's because things like that have been taken away from me.

When it was Claire's birthday, in March, she wanted candles on her cake. Well, why shouldn't she? And

Mum and Dad didn't know what to do, but it was all right in the end because Claire blew out her candles at her party; and of course I would have gone upstairs and hidden away from that lot, anyway. So I sat upstairs in my room waiting for them to sing "Happy Birthday to You" so I'd know the candles were all safely out; and I was so angry that I cried — but only with my right eye, because the left one doesn't produce tears much now.

So that's it, Stevie. All right. Now I begin to see how I can use you. I will show you the way, Stevie. My way. This way.

I'm going to get over it. And no one knows how I feel — except Daniel, of course, who knows everything. He enjoys watching people suffer. That's why he asked me to set something on fire. He knew I wouldn't be able to do it.

But I can, Stevie. I will show you what to do. I am not afraid.

That evening I lay on my bed and I thought, maybe, now that I had the devil's toenail, if I had lots of time and no one was hassling me, maybe I could manage it. Strike a match. If I was outside I could drop it and stamp on it really quickly and it would be all right. And maybe, you never knew, I might even be able to set something alight. A piece of paper. If I weighed it down with stones it would be quite safe. And then I might even be able to be with people who were smoking without having to sit on my hands so no one could see how much they were shaking.

And then you can go on to bigger things, Stevie.

And then perhaps I might be able to set something bigger on fire. Get into the gang, no trouble.

And no one could blame you, Stevie.

And no one could blame me.

I mean, I'd just be getting my own back, wouldn't I?

22

The grocers on the corner by the main road keeps its matches behind the counter, but the woman at the cash register gave them to me, no trouble at all. Well, I look quite old . . . and being scarred helps. People are afraid of me, you see, and sorry for me, and curious about me, and revolted by me; and they're afraid of saying anything in case it comes out wrong. The woman gave me the box of matches, and the last thing she was going to say was, *Be careful not to burn yourself.*

We went down to the old brickworks, the devil's toenail, the matches, and I. The matches were in my pocket to start with, but I kept worrying they'd catch fire so I took them out and held them in my hand. They rattled every time I went over a bump in the road. And even when I got off my bike they rattled because I couldn't stop myself from shaking.

I know matches can't burst into flames all by themselves really: but I couldn't help it.

I pulled aside the two loose planks in the fence that no one knows about but me. The sun was easing the chemical smell of creosote out of the wood.

We've got a tin of creosote in our shed at home, and it's got FLAMMABLE on it in big letters. I wish Dad would get rid of it, but of course I haven't said anything. I just don't go in the shed. I don't go near anything with flammable written on it if I can help it. Daniel, he must be a real hazard, what with his body spray and his hairspray and everything. I wouldn't like to have to wear all that stuff. I'm glad he doesn't go on at me all the time about being smelly, like he does Ryan.

Ryan doesn't matter, Stevie. Think about fire.

It isn't until you think about it that you realize how many things can catch fire. There were a couple of abandoned sheds over by the rust-crusted gates. They were old and so dry they'd go up like fireworks: it'd only take one dropped match in the gap between the grass and the floorboards. I could hide a long way away and watch it.

And that'd be fun, Stevie.

Watch little people coming to try to put it out. I'd watch them, jumping and small, like cartoon characters, and it would be funny.

And then you'd have power over them, Stevie.

And then I'd have power over them, and perhaps I'd not be afraid of fire anymore, and the dreams would go away.

They say you can smell fear: well, I don't want to stink anymore. You can understand that, can't you?

You'll be a new person, Stevie. Trust me.

There was a rusty freight car over by the old railway line. It was filled with broken bricks and torn bits of screwed-up newspaper. I took a piece of newspaper out. There was no one around.

I walked along carefully until I found a place where the fence turned a corner and sheltered me. I weighed the ends of the newspaper down with bits of brick.

That's the way, Stevie.

Matchboxes are fiddly even when your hands aren't shaking. The tray stuck, and then I pushed it too hard and all the little matches fell down among the chinks of broken concrete. For a moment I thought I'd lost them. Hoped I'd lost them.

Look, Stevie. There they are.

But they were still there. I picked each one up very carefully between finger and thumb and dropped it delicately back into the box.

Have you ever looked at a match? I mean, really looked at one?

You know, I saw an adder once, and I couldn't believe that such a little thing could cause such harm. Matches are like that. One small match, thrown at someone who had petrol in his hair.

We didn't mean to hurt anyone, they said. *We were just messing around.*

I picked up a match by the very very end.

23

On the tenth try there was a scrape and a tiny roar and a flame; but my hand was shaking so much I shook it out again.

Well done, Stevie: but give your fear to me. I can use it.

But it was all right. Even that much was something, and I'd got the hang of it now. Hold the match really tight. Lay it along the side of the matchbox and then whisk it away from you. And the friction lights it.

There. Look at it. Flames, going up.

I wonder what I'd looked like all those months ago, with the flames going up from me. No one had stayed to watch. It was a pity, really, a waste; but they'd all run away. I suppose they were scared. And then there were other people running towards me, but none of them stopped to watch, either. Not that I was taking a lot of interest in anyone else at the time: but no one in court said *I saw everything that happened.*

I dropped the match onto the newspaper. It sat there for a little while, made a charred mark, and went out.

Yes. That was because flames go up, not down.

Now something bigger, Stevie.

All right.

I bent the newspaper into a bridge shape and squashed the ends down with big chunks of concrete. Then I was ready to burn something. To destroy something.

There was still no one about, not anywhere, except for a sparrow hawk that slid through the air over my shoulder and made my insides lurch and then flop back in a cold tangle.

People say, *It's all in the past*: but the past leaks.

It's like the time Claire left a red paper napkin up her sleeve. Everything in the wash came out blotched with pink. I've still got a pair of pink pants that I only wear on weekends when no one's going to see them.

That's my life: everything blotched and spoiled and hidden away, for shame.

So give it to me, Stevie: I want it.

And suddenly I got out the devil's toenail and I held it up to my face, really close so I could breathe in the warmth of it. And I spoke to it. Spoke to it out loud, because I didn't care anymore.

"Take it," I said. I almost shouted it. "It's all yours, all right? Take it and do what you want with it. I don't want it anymore."

And suddenly it was as if the air had become much thinner, because I could move so easily. As if I'd grown wings, or become ten times stronger. I could watch my hands doing things and it was as if someone else was working them.

My hands lit another match, let it flare, and then pushed it under the newspaper. And left it there. It took a long time for anything to happen. And then, just as the paper was turning black and tissue-thin, a picture on it caught my eye. It was of a bloke in a suit — just that, just a bloke. I don't know who he was: he might have been a politician. He had that look about him.

A stream of breeze slipped round the fence and a flame bounced and licked out from under the newspaper. And then — flick — it wasn't a flame, but a fire. A fire burning up through that gray suit, that gray face.

And suddenly I wanted to end it — to stamp and stamp on the fire until the last glimmer was ground down and utterly defeated.

But my body wasn't doing what I told it. So all I could do was watch.

The man smiled even when the flames were biting through him. He smiled until the fire had turned him to ash and blown him to nothing on the wind.

When it was all over I turned away and walked blindly over to the fence, and I was sick.

24

When I'd finished throwing my guts up I crouched down and shivered for a while.

You've done well, Stevie. Very well. That's a good start.

Then I got on my bike and rode back to the grocers by the main road where no one from Farmstate or Highford would ever go. I wanted to buy some lighter fluid. Oh, and a bar of chocolate, to celebrate.

You see *I'd struck a match:* and that was really something.

Of course it is, Stevie: a whole new beginning. Now you aren't useless anymore; and I will be able to use you.

When I was first in the hospital I wanted to die. It was partly the pain, but it was mostly guilt — guilt for being the sort of person people wanted to set on fire.

But then Mum moved into the hospital, and she wouldn't go away, and she kept talking about stepping-stones. Every day she'd decide I'd made some little bit of progress and tell me I'd got on to another stepping-stone and she kept saying, *How wonderful, well done;* and even though I knew it wasn't true it stopped me from wanting to die all the time.

I've only been wanting to die sometimes for quite a while; and even when I do, then I've learned to look forward to feeling better again.

It works sometimes.

But that match — well, I suddenly started believing that those stepping-stones were leading somewhere.

Of course, Stevie. I'm not going to waste you. I'm going to have fun. Just relax and keep believing.

It was the devil's toenail, you see. I could put my trust in it. That's all I had to do.

I said that the past leaks: well, that's true; but that match was in the past, too, now, in the past indelibly forever.

I put the lighter fluid on the counter in front of the woman at the cash register, and as I did a large person who smelled of Mum wafted up behind me. Made me jump a mile. And it had never even occurred to me that the place was just round the corner from Mum's office, had it?

When she saw the lighter fluid she didn't know what to say. So she made a huge effort and said, ever so ever so stupidly playfully:

"Heavens, what is that for, Stevie?"

She's the enemy, Stevie: get rid of her.

I didn't know what to say either, except *What are you doing here?* but somehow I found myself going for the withering sarcasm:

"Dinner," I said. But Mum didn't realize it was sarcasm, and she started talking at a hundred and fifty miles an hour.

"What a nice idea," she said, gabbling. "We'll have a barbecue. It's lovely weather, and I'm picking Claire up from Katie's at four. A nice *vegetarian* barbecue. Won't that be lovely?"

Mum keeps up this pretense that I'm not round the bend. I suppose she's too embarrassed to admit it.

Get rid of her, Stevie!

I tried to put her off, but of course with Mum you can't get a word in edgeways.

"We can have some prawns — Claire likes prawns — and toast. Cheese on toast. Grilled tomatoes. I might even have some veggie burgers in the freezer. How about baked potatoes? I could start them off in the microwave. That would be nice."

And on and on, until somehow she'd paid for the lighter fluid and a carton of milk — *We've run right out at the office* — she didn't mention meat, but the way she rambled on you'd have thought that it had never crossed her mind.

Dad was dead chuffed to find the barbecue out when he got home, even though he thought he might be coming down with a bout of kidney failure. He really fancies himself as a barbecue cook: he's got this chef's hat, and an apron printed with a bra and garters.

Of course Claire said, *But I thought we weren't allowed to have barbecues anymore since Stevie got burned?* But Mum shushed her and the subject was whisked away as if it had never been mentioned. The nearest Dad got to referring to it was when he said, *Stevie can always go for a walk if he gets bored.* And with Mum and Dad around squabbling busily over the barbecue everything was so totally ordinary and everyday that I didn't get the chance to concentrate on the devil's toenail at all.

So we had the barbecue, and it was OK, really, except that I didn't want the prawns put on the fire. I know it was stupid, because they were dead, anyway; but they looked like babies' fingers, and I just didn't. But it didn't matter, because they were ready-cooked and so we ate them cold. And after we'd eaten everything we sat and watched Claire pretending to fly her broomstick round the garden by jumping from the sandbox to the patio to the back step without touching the ground.

And just once Mum and I looked at each other: but neither of us said anything.

25

I was really stuffed full after the barbecue, so I took my bike out for a ride. Just an ordinary bike ride, that was all; and I wasn't thinking about anything but riding off my dinner.

Come, Stevie. Come and see what my power can do. Come and see what fun it is now you've given yourself to me.

And I don't know how it was, but somehow I forgot to think about where I was going, and when I woke up I found I was only just across the park from the bench.

The gang was there. I swerved quickly into a bush and waited for a chance to sneak off.

Matt was balancing along the back of the bench.

Once Daniel called Matt an alien, and Matt said, *Yeah, I'm the one with the incredible sucker feet,* and then Matt jumped up on the bench and balanced all the way along the back. And that shut Daniel up, and he didn't call Matt names anymore.

Don't let them see me, I said to the devil's toenail. But then I looked over at the gang again — and then again — and Daniel wasn't there. No, he really wasn't: Ryan was sitting on the grass like a giant abandoned onion, but there was no sign of Daniel at all.

Make Daniel go away, I'd said to the devil's toenail. *Make Daniel go away. Make Daniel go away.*

It had worked. I'd asked the devil's toenail to get rid of Daniel, and it had done it. To *Daniel*.

Trust me, Stevie.

I was so completely amazed that when Matt looked across I forgot to duck out of the way, and he saw me. So he waved, and then the others looked round, and then of course I had to ride across to join them.

Jack looked even more like a weasel than ever.

"Hey," he demanded, "what were you doing hiding behind those trees?"

But Matt said, "Look at Jack's dinner," while I was floundering about for an answer.

There was an open lunch box on the grass. At first I thought it was filled with lettuce, but then I looked again and saw a bit of licorice in there as well: and then I looked again, and it was a slug.

"You keep your nose out of there. That's top secret,

that is," said Jack. "That's my stable." And he threw out his puny chest importantly.

"What?"

Matt got back up on the bench and prepared to walk along the back again.

"Of racing slugs," he explained. He sounded perfectly serious, but I could tell he was finding it hilarious.

I looked in the box. Yes, there was more than one. They were the really big fat black ones.

"Have they got names?" asked Ben; and we all turned to look at him because he hardly ever said anything.

"Yeah," said Jack, but I could tell he was lying. "Look, you see that orange stripe along the side? That means it's a proper racing slug, that does. You have to feed them lettuce to get them into racing condition."

Matt made a *he's a lunatic* face at me over Jack's head.

"You should feed them curry," I said. "That'd get them running all right."

And we laughed.

"We could make a racecourse," said Matt. "If we got a milk container out of the recycling bin and cut it down the middle, we could make a pit stop out of the handle."

But Ryan shook his head.

"They didn't ought to run about after a meal," he said.

"Yeah," said Jack, "and that's why you can't run. It's never more than five minutes since you've been stuffing your face."

Ryan started to laugh, but Matt jumped off the bench, rolled Jack over, and stuffed grass down his neck. It was really funny.

Later, when I was cycling home with Matt, I asked him where Daniel was.

"France," he said. "Karting."

Make Daniel go away.

Wow. Wow, it'd really really worked, all the way to France. And I mean, to do things to Daniel — well, that meant the devil's toenail was *really* strong.

Wow, if it could do that to Daniel — to *Daniel* — it could do anything.

As I turned into my road, it was as if a small voice spoke to me through the ticking of my bike.

So, what next? it said.

I was indicating with one hand and the other was on the handlebars, so I wasn't even touching the devil's toenail. But I was almost sure I heard its voice.

So, what next?

26

That evening I caught a glimpse of myself in the bathroom mirror — I'd turned the mirror in my bedroom round, but the bathroom one was bolted to the wall — and, I don't know if it was just because it was quite dark, but I sort of recognized myself. What I mean is, the eyes in the mirror looked back at me, and they didn't despise me.

I'd forgotten what that was like.

I slept really well, and in the morning I turned my bedroom mirror round and looked at myself again: at *myself*. And there I was. Bald, and burned — but still somehow myself.

I stared at myself for ages. I think it was the first time since before.

And I thought, OK, so I've got to set the library bin on fire before Daniel will let me into the gang. Well, that's no problem, not with the devil's toenail. I've proved that.

That'll be a surprise for Daniel, that will.

What will Daniel do when he finds out that I've changed? What will he do when he finds out I've got power, too?

Power: that was what it was all about. I had the devil's toenail, and Daniel —

It was partly that Daniel was rich and good-looking, but it wasn't just that. I mean, he could get Ryan to do anything he wanted. Not that good old Ryan wouldn't do anything for anyone, of course — I mean, he'd always been a real help telling me where things are at school: but it was with Daniel that you noticed it because Daniel got him to do things that no one else dreamt about.

Sit. Stay. Beg. Haven't you heard of deodorant? Roll over, smell-ball.

And Ryan laughed. Rolled about and laughed until he could hardly breathe.

Didn't Ryan ever go home and wonder what Daniel would tell him to do next? Didn't he ever worry if he really did smell?

So there I was. Not hating myself.

Of course not. Because I am magnificent, and you are becoming like me.

And then I thought some more about Daniel, and Ryan, and I thought, *Who would I rather be?*

That was easy:

Daniel.

Obviously.

And I had this expanding, exciting feeling inside me. Now that I had the devil's toenail's power, then I really could be like Daniel. I wasn't afraid anymore, so I could do anything.

So what did I want to do? What, in all the world?

What I tell you, Stevie.

Something to prove who I was. Something to prove I was cool, like Daniel. Something I got something out of. Yes.

I got out the devil's toenail, and rubbed my thumb on it, and for the first time I sort of felt I understood it. Yes.

OK. I could do anything.

Something for me, then.

What did I want?

27

I told you about Craig, didn't I, the one who wears a blazer and wants to be an accountant?

Yes, that's right, him.

Well, I went round to his house once or twice after school and once he took me up to the attic and showed me his train set.

It went round the whole attic. He had four engines, and sidings, and all sorts of stuff, and he had this thing so that when the mail car went over this bit of track, a little mailbag popped out and got caught in a net on the platform. At least that was what was supposed to happen, but of course you had to do it fifteen times before it worked properly. Craig wouldn't let me touch anything in case I broke it.

I only went once or twice. He got up my nose a bit, and no one likes him all that much. And train sets are juvenile and pathetic, aren't they?

In any case, Dad said there wasn't room in our attic for a train set.

The point is, that was ages ago. Before the devil's toenail. When I *wanted* a train set.

I can hardly believe it now: I can hardly believe it was me. I mean, train sets aren't any good for anything, are they? And now, if I wanted something, I had the strength to go and get it — and that meant I didn't have to make do with Craig or his train set. And why shouldn't I have what I wanted?

Pride goeth before destruction, Stevie; though it does make the journey somewhat easier. What shall you do? Something dangerous, I think. And extremely entertaining.

Taking things from shops was just making things difficult for yourself, what with the alarms and mirrors and nosy shop assistants and whatever. But people's houses — that was easy. It was dead easy in the hot weather, particularly: I could go round the old people's bungalows. Because, I mean, half of them are blind, and those bungalows get so roasting hot in summer people have to leave their doors and windows open or die of heatstroke. And a lot of the people living in them were bound to be barmy, like Ben's old nan, who went out to the butcher's in her slip the other day and then refused to pay him because she said he was trying to take advantage of her.

OK. So that's what I do, then.

Excellent, Stevie.

Well, why shouldn't I?

28

It was swelteringly hot. Dad was at work and Mum had taken Claire and her friend Katie swimming.

I don't go swimming anymore. Don't want to. It used to be because people might not want to be in the water with me, but now I just don't want to: particularly not with Claire. Particularly not with Claire and Katie, who giggle all the time. I don't suppose it *is* about me, always. But sometimes it feels as if it is.

So it all worked out fine. Yeah. When I rubbed my thumb round the ridges of the devil's toenail I heard a friendly voice whisper, ***You'll be all right with me to look after you, Stevie!*** And I suddenly discovered that I was more comfortable inside than I'd been for ages.

This way, Stevie.

I cycled over to the old people's bungalows. I knew them quite well because Nanny lived in one before she had to go into a home.

Not yet, Stevie.

I just rode past: the place was still too busy, it was full of old ladies waddling along towing shopping baskets on wheels and old men hauling themselves out of cheap old cars.

So I rode out of town, and then back through the park, and by that time the place was heavy with a sort of immovable warm-spongy quiet.

Now, Stevie.

Just as I wanted it.

I chained my bike to a barrier that was there to stop cars from ramming into the bungalows and looked at them carefully through the hedge.

Everything under control, Stevie.

I suppose it was knowing the devil's toenail was there, but I was completely relaxed. I walked along the hedge and I knew I wasn't going to be seen: just knew it.

There were a few doors open, but I carried on past them because none of them was the right one. It was like a police lineup, and I knew that I'd recognize my one.

A lineup?

He was scarred all down one side of his face, your honor, and he hadn't got any hair.

Bit of a giveaway, that.

So what, Stevie? You'll be at home in prison. Lots of my lives are there.

But it was OK, because I didn't care. Really, honestly.

The judge would say things about how he understood that I might have a grudge against society, but that even so, the type of crime I had committed could not be tolerated.

But so what?

Mum would be there looking white, just like she had when she'd arrived at the hospital.

Families are the enemy, Stevie. In any case, she only cares about herself. Like everybody else.

But I didn't care about Mum, either. Mum only bothered about *me* because she thought I was still part of herself. I was her son — a sort of a cross between a trophy and a lapdog.

There, said the little voice, and the devil's toenail fizzed strongly under my fingers. *That's the one.*

I paused in my stride for a moment. The bungalow was only two from the end of the row, and those last two had a shut-up, gone-on-holiday look about them.

It was one of those days when you can hear everything really clearly: but all I could hear was a great wide silence punctured by faraway cars swooping along, and a bubbling cooing from some telephone wires across the road in the park.

The thought *turtledove* drifted across my mind. And then I thought *turtledove*? And I looked, and there it was. A turtledove, sitting on the wire, bubbling to itself. My first ever.

See? said the small voice, a little amused. ***Things are going to be great.***

Come into my parlor, Stevie.

Yes. They were going to be great. I stopped by the path.

The door to the little bungalow was wide open; and inside all that was moving was dust, twirling lazily, undisturbed. I walked up to the door.

I could take anything I wanted.

There wasn't a sound, and it was just so easy. Old people, they say, *We used to leave our front doors open in those days.* Old people live in a different world. Times have changed. They've changed so much.

That was what they were going to find out.

I stepped quietly onto the doormat. The place smelled horrible — stale bodies and tobacco. I'd do it really stylishly, slip in and out and no one would know

I'd been there. Until they missed their . . . whatever.
Whatever I fancied.

I could take anything I wanted: *anything I wanted.*

Suddenly it felt like Christmas.

As I took a second step into the stale smell I heard
the little voice again.

It's Christmas every day with me, it said.

29

It was so still in the bungalow you could almost hear the dust falling.

There was a lot of dust.

Straight ahead was a cupboard, a shoddy peeling thing seared by the heat.

That was the first place to look.

One step, two steps, pressing down on the thread-bare carpet ever so carefully.

Footprints?

It's all right. I'm looking after you.

Using your life, Stevie.

The cupboard door was stiff. Of course, it was old, like all the people who lived here. So. Pull hard . . . and harder . . . brace yourself . . . BANG!

It's all right.

The afternoon is only just beginning, Stevie.

It's all right. Wait.

Wait until your heart has stopped ricocheting off your ribs. Wait until you can breathe.

Now . . . look.

Glasses.

Glasses?

And . . . a chipped bowl.

And . . . nothing. Nothing else.

Damn.

That's right, Stevie: damnation. Quite soon.

Nothing else except a loud sigh.

What?

Jump up, smash your knee, whisk round.

There. Behind the door.

There. There. There. There. There. There. There. There.

I clutched my knee and hopped up and down, and the only reason I managed not to yell out was because he was still asleep.

He was pink and fat inside his string undershirt, like a leg of pork. He was lolling back, mouth open. Over in the corner were the bat folds of a wheelchair.

Silly old *fool*! Didn't he know what the world was like? Sitting there with his door open and his wallet on the table.

His wallet, Stevie. His wallet. His wallet.

My feet took a step forward without my brain having to give them any orders.

That's it, Stevie.

I had to reach across the flabby dome of his stomach to get it. He smelled horrible — tobacco and sweat and pee. I picked up the wallet and as I did something fell down with a soft thump onto the floor. I jumped a mile, but he didn't move. He lay like a great pig. I could have cut his throat if I'd wanted to.

Of course you can, Stevie. But not quite yet. Let's have some more fun with you first.

Just for a moment I felt like Daniel.

The wallet was greasy, fat, opened at the end. It stank, and it was strangely bulky. I thought there must be a whole roll of notes inside.

Inside . . . inside there was something dark and moist.

What?

Tobacco.

Tobacco: *damn!*

Not a wallet, a tobacco pouch. Of course, I could see it was now.

I hated feeling such a fool: hated it.

All right. He'd asked for it. I'd trash the stupid place.

And then I'd wake him up, give him a scare, and be away before he'd worked out what was happening. That'd show him.

That's right, Stevie. Good boy. The bedroom first.

Yes, of course. The bedroom. I'd make it so he never went in there without remembering me and what I'd done.

I went through the door to the back part of the bungalow. There was a door to the left.

The bloke coughed as I was opening it. Then he coughed again, and again, and the springs of his chair groaned.

If he opened his eyes he'd see me. So. Into the bedroom, pinch something, out of the window.

It was going to be easy.

I slipped through the door, quickly, quickly, and let it close ever so ever so gently behind me.

And found myself staring at the loo.

30

The old bloke was still coughing — not a feeble, sleepy cough, either, but a waking-up, good-clear-out one.

There was a short yellowing bathtub and a small yellowing washbasin. The loo. A window.

A bedroom window wouldn't have caused me any trouble, I'd have been out of that in no time; but this window was all little panes of ugly dented glass. The only one that opened looked exactly big enough for me to get stuck in. The frames were metal.

The bloke was moving. I could hear him. What if he needed the loo? Old blokes have to go all the time. He might only need the wheelchair for outside. Or it might belong to someone else — someone asleep in the bedroom.

What was I going to *do*?

The bloke was coughing again. Coughing and coughing. Then he started banging. Vicious, it sounded.

Some of those old blokes *are* vicious: they forget we're civilized these days and they go for you with a stick.

Oh, *damn*.

What could I do? What could I do?

Panic, Stevie?

What could I do?

Run: that was the only thing. That old bloke was too fat to run. As long as I ran straight out — jumped if he tried to trip me — I'd be all right.

He'd recognize me, though. Of course he would. There wouldn't be anyone else in the whole area who looked like me. He'd only have to say that I was burned down one side of my face and they'd find me in a couple of milliseconds.

What could I do?

Like a headless chicken, Stevie. Most amusing.

A towel. Over my head.

I grabbed at a towel — blue and mustard — and put it over my head. My reflection stared back at me in the spotty mirror, and just for a moment I was back in Mrs. Woolfit's nursery room playing Third Shepherd in the Nativity play.

And they were sore afraid.

Oh hell, this was ridiculous.

The bloke outside was retching his guts up. Perhaps he'd drop dead.

No, that would be even worse.

Or go to sleep again.

But I couldn't wait. Any moment now his old wife might be waddling home desperate for a pee and she'd come face-to-face with a scar-faced intruder.

I found myself turning round and round, like a squirrel in a trap. To the too-small window, to the door, to the window, to the door . . .

I thought about keeping calm, but I knew there was no point. No point, because there was no way out.

What could I say? The police would come, and they'd talk to me.

Always entertaining, that, Stevie.

That's nothing, of course, I don't care about the police, as long as there aren't too many of them. I'm not too good in crowds. . . .

Oh God, I wish I'd never done it! If you'll only get me out of this, I'll —

"Hello!"

That was the old bloke shouting: not loud, because his throat was clogged up. But who was he shouting *to*? He couldn't know about me, could he?

What could I *do*?

"Hello! HELLO!"

His voice was stronger, now, and urgent. He *must* know about me. Should I run out straight away before he attracted anyone's attention?

Of course I should.

But I stayed, hopping from one foot to the other, and I was dizzy because all the things I knew I ought to do were swirling round with all the things I didn't dare do: and they were all the same.

The chair creaked again, violently.

"HELLO!" he shouted. "HELLO! Is there anyone out there? Help! Help!"

And then he shouted something else. He shouted:

"FIRE!"

And then suddenly there was a balloon blocking my throat so I couldn't breathe. And I was down, down on the ground, pulling at my knees, trying to shrink. Trying to shrink away from the flames.

"Help me," I said.

I'm not sure if there was an answer; but somewhere a long way away I thought I might have heard laughter.

31

 "Fire!"

Silence. It was a hot midafternoon in an old people's complex and everyone was asleep.

"HELP! FIRE!"

And then I smelled it: a wisp of something coming under the door, and with it the smell of bonfire.

Bonfire.

When I was small Dad had an incinerator in the garden, and we used to go out on still nights and set fire to all the old leaves and stuff.

Suddenly I was back to being nine, all excited at being out in the dark, playing Robin Hood. I had a green sweatshirt: I used to wear that.

And suddenly I was grabbing the towel from the floor. Putting it in the bathtub. Water. Lots of cold water, until it was heavy and sodden. And the other towel, too. They sent rivulets of water all over me, all over the floor, but that didn't matter. Nothing mattered but hurrying.

I snatched the door open, but everything out there was a curtain of shifting gray. And then the acrid smoke seized me, clawed its way into me, and squeezed my chest.

Close the door, Stevie! Close the door. You can't breathe.

It was closed before I'd had time to think; but that didn't help much because now there was smoke, thick and white as Christmas, curdling its way under the door.

Then in the flat silence there was a little noise — not much more than a whispering — a chuckling, almost. It took me a couple of seconds to work out what it was.

It was the sound of the beginning of a fire: the sound as the smoldering embers are just flicking into flame and taking on a life of their own, flaring and dancing like tiny devils.

Hands that weren't really mine fumbled at the window and opened it. And I was breathing clear sweet air, lungful after lungful, even though, at the back of my mind like the ticking of a time bomb, I knew that the open window was sucking the smoke in after me.

Help me, I thought.

And then I said it out loud.

"Help me. Help me."

But the only answer came from outside: a rumble and a double thump. And I knew, as if I'd seen it, what had happened. The old man had fallen trying to get up. He was lying on the faded carpet as the flames burned.

The fire was more than a chuckle now. It was cracking, cackling, spitting. What was burning? The curtains, the carpet? The foam from the old armchair that breathed poison as it burned?

I turned back to the door. I had to get out.

Stay, Stevie. This is fun.

Now! I thought. But somehow it was as if my hands weren't mine anymore, and my feet were backing me away.

It was as if there was a barrier across the room so I couldn't move. I couldn't. I couldn't.

Then something outside smashed, horribly loudly. All my insides lurched in different painful directions.

A window: broken, or shattered in the heat?

If I went out now I'd be able to save both of us. Grab his feet and pull him along the ground.

I wanted to do it. I really wanted to do it.

"I need to get out," I said; but all the time I was pressed against the washbasin as far from the door as I could be. And I couldn't make myself move. I tried, but I just couldn't move.

And then there were voices. I couldn't hear them properly because of the white noise of the fire, but there was more than one. Questioning, they were; and coarse with age; and then sharp and exclaiming.

And then it was too late to get out.

I found myself sitting on the floor. There was nothing I could do now; and before me passed a procession of things: what-will-be, and what-might-have-been. The what-will-be was easy: discovery, police, whatever, whatever, trial, blah-blah-blah. But the might-have-been fractured endlessly, like light through shattered glass: a million different paths, a million decisions.

And there I was. Me and the devil's toenail.

And you've turned out fun at last, Stevie.

There was a thumping from somewhere very close. Old people. There were fat old people, out in the front room, helping the old bloke. Not like Superman, not like heroes. They'd have elasticated stockings or up-to-the-armpit trousers. Shiny brown shoes. Hairnets. Doggedly foolishly obstinately helping.

There were two and a bit more bumps and then more voices. A bumping, coughing, confusion.

Then there was another voice, even nearer, just out-side the window.

"They've sent for the ambulance and the fire engine," it said. "It was his pipe, you know. It'd dropped down on the carpet. Ever so easily done."

I felt as if someone had thumped me in the stomach. He'd dropped his pipe? Oh, no, he hadn't: I'd done it. I'd knocked it down when I was reaching for his tobacco pouch. I'd heard it fall. It was me that'd set the place on fire. That old bloke might have been burned alive and I'd never have known what I'd done.

Burned alive.

Burned dead.

Which is what we wanted, Stevie, remember?

I got the devil's toenail out of my pocket. I think I might have been going to get rid of it — flush it down the loo — but as I held it the warmth of it sent a glow through me.

Stevie, Stevie. This is what you wanted, wasn't it? What you asked me for. Power to do things.

Setting a house on fire.

Setting a *house* on fire.

And suddenly I realized it was what I'd wanted. Power, you see. All those old people — the bungalow —

134

the ambulance, the fire engine, all coming and running because of me.

Because of *me*.

Ambulance. Fire engine. Police.

Police.

I held the toenail close to my face. Focused on it.

All right, I thought. *I've got what I came for. Now, if you're so great, get me out of this.*

And as soon as I said it, it was as if someone drew up a blind inside my head and I saw things I hadn't noticed before. I saw that the smoke that had been curling dense as sheep's fleece under the door had dissipated into smeary dullness. And the crackling fire was quiet.

I opened the door. Outside the place was hung with foggy smuts and hazed with gold. The door opposite was black and oily, but there was nothing stopping me going out. Something inside my head said *towel*, so I dropped it off my shoulders, all wet, on the floor. That would puzzle someone. I found myself smiling at the thought.

There was a bedroom behind the door opposite. An ordinary bedroom with an old-fashioned eiderdown and brushes on the dressing table. I trod softly across the faded rugs.

Outside there were voices. They got louder as I opened the window, but there was no one in sight.

I had to leave the window open behind me — but already there were sirens in the distance, clashing against each other, and there wasn't time to worry. So I slipped across the handkerchief lawn and over the silly wooden fence and suddenly everything was soft and green. And instead of the harsh clattering of old voices there was a bubbling; and it was a turtledove.

I sank down into the long grass at the edge of the park and breathed deep of the soft clean air.

32

No one came to find me. No one knew I was there, or had ever been there.

Sirens.

Not for me. Not for me. Not for me.

That was all that mattered.

The sirens were harsh; but just before they got unbearable, they stopped, and doors slammed, and there were official faraway voices. And then, ages later, the heavy vehicles drove away again, but with their sirens quiet.

I cycled the long way home through the back lanes so I wouldn't meet anyone. I felt happy. Mum and Claire had got back from swimming and Claire told me an incredible story all about a fire engine and a police car and an ambulance, and how they'd seen them putting somebody into the ambulance from a house right near Nanny's, but Mum wouldn't let Claire go close enough to see what was wrong with him.

"We saw some smoke, though," said Claire, proudly. "It was ever so smelly. But the man wasn't dead," she went on, with regret, "because he was sitting up in this chair-thing that the ambulance men were carrying. Someone said that he'd set his bungalow on fire."

I kept my mouth shut, but something inside me was very happy. Triumphant.

"Mummy, do you think that if I hurt myself the ambulance men might give me a ride in one of those chair-things?"

Mum suddenly sniffed.

"*You* smell of smoke, Stevie," she said; but I wasn't worried. I just said something about smelling some smoke myself when I was going past the park.

I don't think Mum believed me, quite. But she couldn't prove anything, and so that was the end of that. I wandered off to the bathroom to make sure I hadn't got any obvious streaks of ash about me, and as I was splashing cold water over my head I heard a little voice.

See? it said. ***I am designing you a great life, Stevie.***

And I looked back, and I realized it was true. Things had been a bit hairy at times, but if I'd only trusted the devil's toenail instead of panicking then everything would have been fine. As smooth as butter. As smooth as Daniel. Yeah. I mean, I'd done some neat stuff. And everything had turned out great.

Thanks, DTN.

Oh, I enjoyed it, Stevie.

33

 Friday.

Could have been worse: could have been double PE with Mr. Furness. He's got really hairy legs and thinks anyone who doesn't like hurdling is abnormal.

"Do we *have* to go away again tomorrow?" I asked, hung heavily over my cereal. Mum was dashing round putting stinky stuff down the sink and wiping things and she was making my head hurt.

"You know we are, Stevie. That's why we've kept the camper."

"I don't see why I can't —"

"Claire! Have you got your shoes on? Good girl."

And they bundled out, all happy because they were going clothes shopping.

There's no accounting, is there?

Friday. Oh, yes, of course, I remember. It was the last day I was going to be at home over half term, wasn't it?

And you know what happens on the last day of a school holiday.

That's right.

Homework.

I mean, it's really stupid giving out homework over the holidays. They say *A change is as good as a rest*, but if they give you homework you don't get either, do you? Well, Daniel would be coming back from his karting holiday all fresh and lovely because he'd had a change; but the rest of us were stuck. Not that I do homework, much, obviously, but you know what it's like. You get the dried-up old teachers who dish out automatic detentions if it's not handed in: and the last thing I wanted to do was be in Farmstate School a second longer than I had to.

So I did my French. It's such a mess, French, isn't it? All run-together honking. Of course, what I *should* have done is put a curse on my French teacher; but I was so used to feeling resentful and bored doing homework that it didn't occur to me until it was too late to bother. Anyway, Mr. Plumfield's already cursed with six-year-old twin girls — I mean, that's like *Claire squared* — and that's enough misfortune for anyone.

Friday.

Yes, after lunch I had to mind Claire again while Mum went into the office. The devil's toenail whispered something about money in my ear, and when I passed the idea on to Mum she agreed to pay me with hardly any fuss at all. It was really neat being able to get people to do what I wanted.

Power, Stevie. It makes things much more fun. And you are going to do lots of amusing things before you die.

I was feeling quite pleased with myself: but then along came Claire and spoiled everything.

The first thing she did was cut through the clothes-line with scissors and tread half Dad's shirts into the vegetable bed. I'd only turned my back for a minute. And then she flew her broomstick off the sandbox and went and smashed the old milk bottle Dad uses to mix weed killer in. And *then*, of course, she took the opportunity of me being occupied picking up the pieces to tear one of my cycling magazines. The little swine did it just as Mum was coming through the door, as well — which was lucky for Claire, because there were all sorts of things I would have done to her, otherwise. You know, the sort of things that could be passed off as accidents. The devil's toenail was really quite clever and inventive. But Claire — it was crazy, but she was such a complete, perpetual pain that I didn't have a chance to think about the devil's toenail properly until after dinner.

She's made a fool of you, Stevie. You can't let her get away with it.

I want revenge on Claire, I whispered to it, concentrating very hard.

That was all I asked for. Revenge. Justice. What's wrong with that?

Sounds fun to me, Stevie.

34

The bench where the gang hangs out is only five minutes from home on my bike. Everyone knows that bench belongs to us. It belongs to the gang, I mean. I *have* seen little kids sitting on it in the daytime, but only for a dare. And Jack's spray-painted so much obscene graffiti on it that nice people don't sit there anymore.

"Where are your slugs?" I asked, because Jack was whiling away his time clapping his hands on gnats and then inspecting the remains.

"Mum found them," said Jack, offhandedly. "Hey, look, this one's still alive! Look, Matt! It's writhing in agony!"

"No, it's not," said Matt. "That's the wind making its legs move."

"Did your mum scream?" asked Ben, hopefully.

Jack sniggered.

"Yeah. It was brilliant. She threw the whole lot out

into the garden and kept shuddering all over and screeching."

"I bet she hit you," said Matt.

"Couldn't catch me," said Jack, smugly.

Families are really embarrassing: they're the enemy, that's what you have to remember. And Jack's mum is actually more embarrassing than mine. Jack's mum wears high heels and low fluffy tops, and once when I was there she asked Jack if he'd been to do a wee-wee.

But then all mums are embarrassing: except Matt's, of course, his mum's really friendly, and she's got a brilliant figure; and Ryan's mum's great, too — as soon as you go in she starts handing out chips for everybody; and Ben's really lucky because he lives with his nan and she's going a bit potty and keeps giving him cigarettes. And Daniel —

I didn't really know much about Daniel, except that he got expelled from his boarding school. And that he was really really rich. Getting expelled's cool.

Yes, there are worse things, Stevie. As you'll find out.

On the way home Matt asked if I'd like a Saturday job at his dad's market stall. I was so surprised I couldn't answer.

"You have to get up early, but the money's OK, and it's a laugh," he said.

I wanted to say, *No one would buy food that I'd touched.* But instead I said:

"I've got to go away again this weekend with my parents."

"That's OK, Dad doesn't need anyone till next month."

And after that I didn't quite know how to say I wouldn't. So I just said I'd see him on Monday.

"Did you have a nice time?" asked Mum, and I said *Yeah, OK,* which is what I always said. But this time saying it was easy.

A nice evening in the park.

That's because you're powerful, Stevie. That's because you can get people to do as you want.

If only things could stay as they were. I mean, I had power over Ben and Ryan; and Matt had power over Jack, so everything was fine.

If only Daniel didn't ever come back.

Oh, the things I'd have liked to do to Daniel.

I got out the devil's toenail, and as I held it I imagined them all.

In detail.

35

The next morning Dad woke us all up early, which was horrible — well, the rest of us were *tired*. He packed the car while we chomped tiredly at our cereal — *I think I might have thyroid trouble, I feel as if I just can't relax* — and then he bundled us in, all weary as we were, and threw drinks and coats and things on top of us, and then drove off, very carefully, so Claire wouldn't be sick.

Miles and miles. We stopped for a break in a little town, trudging sweatily around until Claire had nagged Mum into buying her a big tube of sweets, and then we drove on again. And on, and on, until Dad steered into a field and Mum said, "Where's this?" and of course it was a bird place. So we all piled out, even hotter and sweatier than ever, and stood about panting.

It's funny, but that's the way life happens, isn't it? You trudge along, bored, and faintly falling in with everybody else; and then something comes along at a hundred miles an hour and you discover you've been walking along the main line.

You see, the devil's toenail came up with something big for me to do. Really big, like Lex Luthor. Or Daniel. It gave me the chance to use my power. The chance to prove what I'm really made of — to myself, do you understand?

I've got to tell the truth. That's what all this is for, to make it easier to tell the truth. To tell the truth to myself.

But I don't think I can do it.

I don't think I can do it.

36

The truth.

OK.

Ready?

The bird place was by the sea, and when we'd got out of the shelter of the trees we found it was really windy. We walked along the cliff path beside the gulls that slid dourly along the wind; and, far, far below us, cormorants whirred along like elastic-band airplanes. Claire was whining and whining because she wanted to look through the big pay telescope: but it was too high for her, and anyway we hadn't got the right change. But still she whined and whined, and stamped, and threw pebbles at our feet, and everyone who walked past looked at us: flabby dad, crumpled mum, deformed boy, and horrible little girl.

And I wanted to push them all over the cliff.

And then Mum got really upset: she was exhausted with trying to keep us all happy, you see. But Dad couldn't see what the problem was because Mum spent her whole life coaxing and flattering and he assumed it was just one of the things women did. So then Mum turned on *him*.

"These holidays are supposed to be for me, too," she snapped, "and what do I do? Spend the whole time trailing round after you three!"

And luckily before Dad could think of anything to say Claire said, "I want to climb on the rocks!"

And Dad hesitated, because the idea of Claire going somewhere else was really appealing.

"It's too dangerous," said Mum, exasperated.

Dad sighed.

"I WANT to climb on the rocks," said Claire. "I want to climb on the ROCKS!"

"All right," said Dad, really stressed. "I'll take you later on, if you're good."

"I WANT TO CLIMB ON THE ROCKS!" said Claire, louder, about to go into full tantrum. And there were all these people about.

"Oh all *right*," said Dad. "I'll come if I must."

Mum glared at him.

"So you're going to go off and leave me again, are you?"

"Well, I can hardly —"

"All you want *me* for is to be your housekeeper and babysitter."

I couldn't stand being with them another minute.

"You stay here with Mum," I said. "I'll take Claire climbing."

Mum made a huge effort, filed her bad temper, and was grateful.

"Be very careful," she said. "Don't take her anywhere unsafe."

"It's all right," said Dad. "Stevie will take care of her."

37

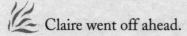 Claire went off ahead.

"Hey!" I shouted. "Not that way, it's too dangerous."

As if I cared.

She stopped and turned round. Her face was all sticky where she'd been wiping sweets all over herself.

"So what?" she said, daring me to stop her.

The trouble with Claire is that Mum and Dad don't believe in hitting her. There were loads of people about, anyway.

So I tried reasoning with her: not that that's got much of a history of working.

"You'll fall off and kill yourself."

There's a thought, Stevie.

"No, I won't. I never fall off. So there!"

Make her go this way, Stevie. This way. Over here.

I tried a different sort of reasoning.

"But there's loads of people over there. That's where they go to watch the birds," I said.

She pulled down the corners of her mouth and made her eyes go crossed.

"*Pooey, pooey, pooey.*"

"And if you go over there you'll see loads of them. Hundreds and hundreds of birds, all round you."

Claire hesitated.

"Anyway, the cliffs are for grown-ups. Anyone can get up there, even grannies. Let's go this way. It's just as high, and it's miles more difficult."

Good, Stevie. Somewhere lonely.

It was easy, though, really. The rocks were scratchy, but that meant you didn't slip. I kept as close to Claire as I could, but sometimes there was a clambery bit followed by an easy stretch and then she'd get a few yards ahead.

It was one of those really clear days, bright and fresh. There was a flat plant that smelled sharp when you trod on it. Halfway up we came round into the sun and the rock began to sparkle.

Yes, this way, Stevie.

The last bit was the hardest, and I had to give Claire some help. She was wearing a yellow skirt. Yes, I remember: she was wearing a skirt, and I kept getting close-up views of her grubby underpants.

I gave Claire a boost up the last big slab. I'd let her go first all the way: it was easier.

"Wow!" breathed Claire, standing silhouetted against the sky. "We're right at the top!"

So I scrambled up onto the ledge after her — and looked down.

And down, and down, and down, past jumbled rocks and tiny clumps of tough green, to the sea.

Here, Stevie. This is the place. Stay here.

I sat down quickly. I think my knees gave way a bit. I mean, I don't mind heights, but that was a shock. I hadn't realized the coast turned back on itself, and we'd ended up right at the top of the headland.

At the top of the headland, Stevie, all alone with your sister.

Power. Just what you wanted.

"Come back from the edge," I said. The wind was strong and I was in charge of her.

Of course Claire never does anything I tell her.

"No," she said, and took a step closer.

I wasn't having that. Mum and Dad were a long way away. There was no one for her to hide behind here.

"Sit down," I said; and something of what I was

thinking must have shown on my face, because she plonked herself down.

Revenge, Stevie.

Claire was staring at me, but I did my best to ignore it. She was just a horrible little rat.

"You're really ugly," she said.

I suppose I should be used to that sort of thing, but it took me off guard. Claire wasn't even on the side of me that was burned — I'm careful about not letting that happen.

There's nothing to stop you doing anything you like, Stevie.

"You'd be ugly even if you hadn't been burned," she said.

Go on, Stevie. Anything you like.

I just grunted. The devil's toenail was pressing into me through my pocket. I wanted to hit her; but I didn't. I sat and gazed at the bright sharp sea.

No one could blame you, Stevie.

"I wish you *weren't* so ugly," said Claire. "People keep staring at us. And Kirsty and Sarah won't come to play because they're frightened of you."

I shifted myself so she couldn't see my face, but that

made the devil's toenail dig into me even more. I thought about being powerful. And how high up we were.

Stevie, listen. Listen. This is your chance.

"It's your head," said Claire. "It's ever such a funny shape."

A little voice said to me, *Push her over the edge.*

"Even Mum can hardly bear to look at you," said Claire. "She said so."

I lost my temper. You can't blame me. I didn't do anything to her. Not really. I just told her to shove off — well, I didn't exactly use those words.

Claire stuck her tongue out at me and said she'd tell Mum.

Now, Stevie. NOW!

And then I went to grab her — I was going to clout her, I think — but she ducked, and I missed, and she scrambled to her feet.

And somehow, very quickly — I don't know how it happened, it might have been the wind, or she might have got her feet caught up in that silly yellow skirt — but she staggered, and fell forward, over the cliff.

38

I didn't think what I was doing: it was just like when you knock something over. I threw myself forward and grabbed at the nearest bit of Claire. I got a leg just above the knee. I got a good hold on it, and then I could take a breath. I breathed, and I breathed.

You fool. You fool, Stevie. Let her go.

Claire must have had all the breath knocked out of her, too, because it took her until then to move. She didn't scream — honestly, the one time when she had every reason to scream, and she didn't. But I felt her weight shifting as she tried to push herself back up.

"Stop that!"

Her skirt was gripping the rough rock, but she was slipping inside it. I dug my fingers into her flabby little legs and wondered what I did next. I couldn't see past her backside and I had no idea how she was hanging on.

"Please don't," came Claire's voice.

It was quiet, and not like Claire at all. I would have

told her to shut up, except that she sounded so weird. I wondered if she'd gone and broken her arm again, like that time she hit Kirsty.

"Don't what?"

"Don't push me over the edge," she said.

I opened my mouth to say something: but then my eye fell on a small dark stone lying beside us on the rock. It'd fallen out of my pocket when I'd grabbed Claire, I supposed. I looked at it; I looked at it and looked at it. And I realized that at last I was really powerful.

Can you feel the power singing inside you, Stevie?

I looked all round. There were no boats, no swimmers, no helicopter.

No witnesses.

So let her go, Stevie.

And all I had to do was loosen my grip. No one would know, except me; and it was me who mattered. Then I'd be as big as anyone: as powerful as Daniel.

"Pull me up," said Claire. She sounded really scared.

"Why should I?" I said. "You're horrible. I'd be better off if you did go over."

And, oh, that was true. Yeah. And all I had to do was let go.

158

That's right, Stevie: so do it.

Claire's voice came, thinly, from over the edge.

"I won't be horrible anymore."

I laughed; and I was surprised by how frightening it sounded.

"No," I told her. "You won't."

I lay there, savoring the moment. Power. That was what it was. Power: to do something, be somebody. And that was what I'd been looking for.

"Pull me up. I'll be so good. Please, Stevie."

I didn't want it to end. It was too sweet, too good. I'd remember this, always: one of the best moments of my life.

This is happiness, Stevie. Fulfillment. Self-respect.

"You ruin everything," I said. And I looked at her grubby skirt and her grubby socks and I thought how horrible she was. And she was getting worse: she'd been hell all this last week. She was rubbish. Throwing away was all she was fit for.

You'll be able to watch her fall, Stevie. You'll be able to treasure the memory.

"I know," said Claire. Her voice went faint as the wind whipped it. "But I won't anymore. Pull me up,

Stevie. Please. I've . . . I've only been horrible because I found one of those funny devil's toenails last weekend and I've been pretending it made me evil and nasty."

That was such a shock I nearly did let go of her then: a shock as if my lungs were exploded by bullets of ice. She'd found a devil's toenail and she'd been —

Let her go, Stevie! Now! Let her go!

"I won't do it anymore. Please, Stevie."

But I was frozen. It was like when I'd been in the old man's bungalow.

And I didn't know what my hands were going to do.

39

Let her go, Stevie: let her go, let go.

My hands didn't belong to me anymore, but my brain was churning: round and round, round and round.

Claire had found a devil's toenail and she'd been pretending . . .

No. No. Think of now. Think of all the power we have. Think of her falling. Think of her dying. Think of yourself, Stevie.

I lay there on top of the cliff clutching at my sister's leg with fingers that weren't mine. And it was as if the wind was blowing holes through me: as if I'd somehow faded away until there was nothing real of me left.

But you know I'm real, Stevie. I'm real and strong. And think how much more I can make you do.

Pretending.

Stevie, listen! Listen to me! She's family, don't you know that? She's warping your brain. I have made you a new person.

Pretending.

Stevie, Stevie, listen to me. Listen to me. I saved you. I made you strong.

Pretending, pretending, pretending.

Stevie, listen! You know who I am!

Suddenly I saw the truth. I saw myself. I saw what I'd been doing. And I knew that the devil's toenail was just a stone. Just pretend.

But not me, Stevie. Not us. You know how real we are. Not the devil's toenail, Stevie, but us. You gave your life to me — and I have given you what you wanted.

Just the same as Claire.

Pretending I wasn't burned. Pretending I wasn't bullied.

Stevie, do not be my enemy. Stay and do my bidding and I will make you strong. Stay and do my bidding, or I will —

I thought I heard a little voice coming from deep down inside me. And the voice was hateful, spiteful, cruel, pretend; and so I cast it away from me.

There was something like a scream. A thin wail, trailing away into vast nothingness. Over the edge of the cliff it went, and far, far into the distance.

But that must have been pretend, too. Like nearly all of me.

Playing pretend with a pretty pebble.

Pathetic.

It was the humiliation of it that got to me. And that made me so angry. These last couple of days I'd begun to believe my life wasn't completely spoiled; but all the time it'd all been a pathetic game.

There wasn't much of me left once I'd realized that.

And then my eyes were stinging in the wind, but of course there were no tears. And I was so angry. I seized Claire's waistband and yanked at it and suddenly she was there, on her hands and knees, crimson in the face from hanging downwards. I heaved her away from the edge and dragged her to her feet and shook her.

And then I screamed things in her face. Wild, foul, true things, and they were all whipped away on the wind and blown into shreds.

Claire's red face was all I could see, and I just couldn't stand it. I was so angry I wanted to smash her brains out, pull out her hair, tear her to bits, destroy her. Destroy everything.

So I slapped her. As hard as I possibly could. It echoed

crack-crack-crack round the rocks and it was followed by a little ruffle of yelps. And then I was rubbing my tingly hand on my jeans and just suddenly at last I'd done something right.

I think Claire was too surprised to cry. So I told her things while I had the chance. I told her what she was like. I told her that if she ever said things like that to me again I'd half kill her.

She knew I meant it. She sidled as far away from the edge as she could get and flicked glares at me through her eyebrows. She even opened her mouth once or twice; but she always thought better of saying anything. And I knew I had power over her, even though the power of the devil's toenail was just pretend. I had power over her just like Daniel had power over Ryan: and I was so lonely I wanted to cry.

"We're going back down," I said, just so tired. "Come on."

She did as she was told, for once. I clambered down over those big slabs feeling . . . I don't know. Nothing, really. That was it. I was feeling nothing. Empty. I went down, helping my putrid little sister, and all the time I felt as if I was looking down a well; and it was dark, and dank, and lonely, and deep: and it went on forever.

Halfway down I realized that I must have left the devil's toenail up on the cliff. But so what? I didn't want it. It was all just pretend. Pretend, just like me.

"Stevie," said Claire, when we were back on the path that led down to the car park.

I grunted.

"I didn't know you got cross."

That was so stupid that I roused myself enough to tell her that everyone got cross. But she shook her head.

"No, they don't. Not properly. They pretend not to."

Pretending.

"I do really annoying things, sometimes," Claire went on, as if that was news, "and *still* people don't get properly cross. Like I've been pretending my devil's toenail made me wicked; but everyone keeps on pretending they aren't angry. It's not fair!"

Claire is only six, and really stupid, and not worth talking to; but that caught my attention.

"But *you* were pretending, too," I pointed out.

"I'm little," she said. "I'm allowed to. It's not fair if everyone else does, too. There's Dad pretending he doesn't always have to have his own way, and Mum pretending all she wants is to be a good wife and mother, and you're pretending you don't care they set you on fire."

I didn't know what to say. We walked down the path some more.

"I wish you *had* killed me," said Claire, presently. "I'd quite like to have wings and be able to fly."

"You wouldn't," I pointed out. "You wouldn't go to heaven. You're too horrible."

Claire seemed to consider this.

"So why didn't you let me go over? No one would have known."

I shrugged.

"It was more fun hitting you," I said. Well, it was true.

And then Dad came in sight and Claire ran on ahead to meet him.

They waited for me, but by the time I caught up with them Claire was whingeing and whining because the wind kept blowing her hair in her eyes. Mum came out of the loo in time to say, *Never mind, poor darling.* I sort of slouched along behind, just like someone who'd never even thought of pushing someone over a cliff. Then Claire ran back to me.

"Stevie! The wind keeps blowing my hair in my eyes!"

I remembered what Claire had said about pretending.

"Oh, stop whingeing," I said. "I don't actually care if the wind blows your hair right out, okay?"

And Claire beamed and skipped and ran off to be first back at the car.

And I came last, thoughtfully.

40

So we towed the camper along to a site, and set it up, and then we had something to eat, and then Claire and Dad watched cartoons on the telly. And somehow it was as if I was high up in the sky, like being in the police helicopter that sometimes circles round the houses at night with its searchlight swiveling — and I thought, what a *prat*.

And as I looked down on myself I thought, *Who are you, then?* And that was a new thought. Because if the devil's toenail was only pretend, then all the things we'd done together had really just been me.

I looked back on that week.

Was that me? Was it?

All that time and effort, trying to be cool, trying to be a criminal, trying to be like —

Well, who was it who fancied himself a criminal?

Yes, it was Jack.

I must be mad. I didn't want to be *Jack*.

But . . . up on the cliff. I'd loved it, really loved it: having all that power. For those few minutes I was Daniel. Oh, and it was wonderful.

Supposing I'd let Claire fall. I might have. I'd wanted to: oh, yes, when you've given up your life to a fossilized mollusk it really does things to your personality.

Anyway, supposing I had. What then? I'd have kept it secret. Made something up. Probably. Unless they gave me the third degree and they pried it out of me. And then I'd have ended up in a detention center.

A detention center. Cool, OK?

Oh, yeah. Oh, yeah, that'd have been just lovely, wouldn't it? Like being shut up with the worst people in Highford and never going home.

And suddenly, like the sun coming out, everything seemed crisp and clear. Terribly clear. I saw the gang, and I saw them all as they really were — stupid Jack, and lonely Ben, and lazy Matt. I saw Daniel, and I saw Ryan; and it was as if Ryan was on the top of the cliff, and Daniel was watching him. Biding his time. Licking his lips. Enjoying it.

When you have power you always want to use it.

The truth. It's like those blobby bits you can sometimes see when you've got your eyes closed. As soon as you try to look at them they float away. Always there, but never quite in view.

So I still didn't see everything.

We had fish and chips on the seafront for supper. Claire was quiet, and it was peaceful.

That night, when I was taking my jeans off, I found something in my pocket.

Something made of stone.

But I'd lost that — left it up on the cliff where I'd nearly —

Claire's. That had been *Claire's* devil's toenail, not mine. Mine was here with me. And what I had done with it was real, was part of me indissolubly forever.

All the things I had done. All the things I had felt.

I didn't want to touch it, so I left it in my pocket out of sight.

And I wished it'd been mine that had got left on the cliff.

41

My jeans felt heavy when I put them on the next morning. The weight of the devil's toenail made me feel trapped, diminished, reminded me that I was only myself. I pulled on my T-shirt quickly and did my best to forget it was there.

Mum had cooked breakfast — mushrooms and eggs with fried bread — really old-fashioned food. I know the cool thing to do would have been to sneer at her, but — oh, what was so wrong with it?

Daniel would have sneered — but then Daniel wouldn't have stopped Claire falling off that cliff. Daniel would have sucked everyone dry of sympathy, but all the time he would have been despising them.

"Marmalade?" asked Mum. And it struck me that it must be ever so lonely to despise everybody all the time.

We'd spent half of yesterday getting here, and we had to spend the evening driving home. We were supposed to be leaping up and seizing our holiday pleasure; but we'd all run out of steam.

"We'll just go down to the beach and have a picnic," suggested Mum. "And you can bird-watch from there, Geoff. If you feel well enough."

So Dad went off to get a disposable barbecue and I had a look for the spare bucket and shovel. It wasn't in the car.

"Yes, I'm sure we brought them," said Mum. "Look under the seats in the camper."

I'm too big to be in a camper. I mean, you either have to be a dwarf or wear ice-hockey gear: every time you breathe you hit yourself on something.

The spare bucket and shovel were under one of the benches.

"Good boy," said Mum.

"No, I'm not," I said, automatically. But Mum only laughed at me.

"You boys," she said. "You're all lovely, really, aren't you?"

"No," I said.

"Did I tell you I met Ben in the pharmacy the other day? Oh, and he was so embarrassed because he was buying some things for his nan. He does so much for her."

Well, Ben *has* to keep his nan going, or he'd have to go to live with his dad. That's the only reason he does it.

"And I quite often see Matt taking them things left over from the market stall. He's such a nice boy, too."

Mum's always driveling on like that: gossiping. But that stopped me short, because I thought *Matt*? Because, I mean, Matt was really laid-back and cool.

Wasn't he?

42

We went down to the beach, and among the shingle and pebbles there was actually a patch of sand big enough for me to build this really brilliant sand castle. Took me hours. Claire kicked down one corner while I was off looking for twigs to make the arrow slits. So I went over to her and took hold of her by the front of her T-shirt, and I told her that if she so much as breathed on my castle again I'd dump her in the sea with all her clothes on. And then of course she went away and left me in peace for the rest of the afternoon; and Mum looked at me as if I'd turned into some completely strange person. Which I had.

And I thought that when I got back home I'd go and find the others. And if Daniel still wanted me to set the library bin on fire then I'd tell him he was a prat. And then, if none of the others could be bothered to stand up for me, then I'd go round to Craig's, perhaps, and have another look at his train set. He might even let me touch things once he was sure I wasn't going to smash up his engines.

I imagined it: jumping all over the little models and tiny figures, feeling them go *crunch* under my feet. It was the sort of thing Jack would boast about for weeks, guffawing — *and you should have seen his face* — But that wasn't me. No, not me at all.

I got my devil's toenail out of my pocket and held it in my hand. I could leave it here on the beach, where I'd found it. But it had been important; and it didn't do anything, after all.

"Stevie!"

It was Claire.

"What?"

"Look what I've found!"

It was humped and sluglike on her hand. Yes, that's right, a devil's toenail. That was all we needed, Claire having another fit of being evil. I dug my left hand into a heap of pebbles and squeezed them crossly through my fingers.

And guess what was the last stone I ended up with?

Yep. Right the first time.

Another devil's toenail.

I was a bit affronted. I mean, how many of the blasted things were there? Unless — yes, perhaps there was some dark power in me that attracted them. Something irresistible and strong.

That's it, Stevie. You are full of dark power: follow it.

It could be something genetic, which was why it worked for Claire, as well as me. I was a Time Lord or something.

Follow me, Stevie, and —

"Stevie!" It was Dad, this time, with Mum following.

"Look what we've found!"

Yes, yes, all right, he had three of them. And *Dad* couldn't be a Time Lord: I mean, he was always late for everything.

It wasn't *fair*.

"Spooky, aren't they?" said Mum, poking them.

Huh! I thought, bitterly. I mean, all the trouble I'd been to over the last week, imagining the devil's toenail was really special, and all the time — What a prat.

Unless I was mad.

Then you could do anything, Stevie. And you wouldn't be able to stop yourself. It wouldn't be your fault. Think of it.

Yes, that could be the thing. I was — what'd-you-call-it — where you hear voices, like Joan of Arc —

Who do you want to be, Stevie?

No. That wasn't me.

There I went again.

No. Not a madman. Just a prat.

When I die of terminal boredom, they'll inscribe that on my grave.

HERE LIES STEPHEN GEOFFREY
SAUNDERS: A PRAT

But still, I had enjoyed building the sand castle.

Mum spent the evening cleaning again — well, Grandma's the sort of person who irons creases in her underwear — and Dad and Claire and I went to the arcade to get from under her feet. We lost some money on one of those pincer-grab things, and then Dad had a go on the pinball machine. He's really funny, because he gets all vicious with it. He goes and gets a hundred and fifty trillion points, or something, and gets so carried away he does a victory lap. Yes, really: right round the arcade, while Claire and I stand with our faces to the wall hoping nobody will spot the family resemblance.

When we got back Mum was on her hands and

knees doggedly sweeping the carpet with a dustpan and brush.

"Look," said Dad, tripping over her for the third time, "that much dust couldn't have fallen in a week! You'll be cleaning the pattern off next."

"I don't care," said Mum, sweaty and despairing and hard-done-by.

"Don't worry," I said. "We'll be home tomorrow and then you can have a rest."

"Thank heavens," said Mum.

And she completely failed to realize it had been a joke.

43

We were going home. Home. I sat sweltering in the back of the car and tried to work it out. *I* was going home: but then *I* was a different person from when I'd come. And a whole different person again from a week ago.

I'd stopped hating myself — and that was the main thing — and I'd done it so completely that I'd even stopped trying to be someone else. I mean, I do have my good points. Like . . . er . . . well, I did save Claire's life. That's really something, isn't it? I mean, I can't imagine *Daniel* ever saving anybody's life.

Claire kept squirming about, even though she and lots of Barbies were taking up more than half the backseat as it was. And then she stopped squirming and went all heavy against me and I realized that she was asleep.

It was really disgusting, obviously; but it was better than her going *Are we nearly there yet?* all the time. So I sat really still, and she slept right through us dropping off the camper at Grandma's until we drew up under the orange lamppost outside our house.

I climbed stiffly out of the car onto the hard asphalt of the drive. And there I was, in the real world.

I mean, being away from home — nothing's ever quite real, is it? You're not quite yourself, and life isn't quite life. But as I stood under our lamppost I felt reality all round me, and it was like being in the camper: every time I moved anywhere or thought anything a bit of me hit one of the sides.

I was the wrong shape to fit in with the world; I was too big, too awkward. Daniel was there, and school was there, and there wasn't room for me.

I wanted to get the devil's toenail out and hold it in my hand and say, *Make Daniel go away forever*: but that was no good because it was just pretend. It was pretend and everything else was real. Ever so real.

I was Stephen Geoffrey Saunders, and the power of the devil's toenail was all made up.

I was Stephen Geoffrey Saunders and I'd built a fire, and saved my sister's life.

I was Stephen Geoffrey Saunders and that was all.

And Daniel was Daniel.

44

Ryan was lying along the bench and Daniel was sitting on him. Leaning back ever so comfortably, he was, just so at home.

Jack's head jerked round when he heard my bike.

"Hey, have you seen the door to the clinic?" he demanded.

I had. I'd also recognized the writing.

"You spelled it wrong," I said.

Matt and Ben looked at each other. Well, what I usually did was snigger and say it was really cool; but I'd forgotten I was supposed to be like that.

It seemed ever such a long time since we'd all been there.

"Spelling is an imposition of the elite," announced Daniel.

"Yeah," said Jack, triumphantly. "See?"

I wondered why I'd come, when I was so scared I had

to clutch onto my bike to stop my hands shaking. But I'd wanted to see Matt and Ryan and Ben. And I'd wanted to see what would happen. What would happen in the real world, now that I was me: not me-plus-the-devil's toenail, or me-trying-to-be-Daniel, but me. The one who saved my sister's life.

"He's come begging," said Daniel, pushing himself off Ryan's stomach, which made Ryan cough a bit. "Begging to join us."

Jack brightened.

"Yeah," he said again. "He's got to do his insulation test. What was it?"

His face furrowed with the unaccustomed effort of rubbing his brain cells together until they got hot enough to spark a thought.

"It had to do with the town hall or something," he said, at last.

But Daniel knew, of course: his face was glowing like an angel's.

"Here," he said.

The cigarette lighter shone hard in his hand. Full up, it was, of stuff that flicked into flame so easily . . .

Daniel threw it, and I saw my hand reach out and

catch it without me having to think. And there it was in my hand, satisfyingly heavy, and solid gold. My thumb left a trace of mist as I wiped it over the surface.

"The library!" said Jack, explosively, having finally succeeded in kick-starting a thought process. "That was it, something to do with the library."

And I suddenly realized that Daniel couldn't hurt me: he could only hurt the person I used to be; and he was gone forever.

I stood there and let Daniel enjoy his power. You see, I knew how sweet it was.

Sweet, but short.

"The library's closed," I pointed out, politely; and my hands weren't shaking anymore.

"He's chicken," yelped Jack, in triumph, and started wagging his elbows. "Clerrrrr-uck-uck-uck-uck-uck!"

Daniel's eyes were blazing at me.

"That bin, then. That bin. Now."

I glanced at it. It was made of steel and it was nearly empty apart from a couple of drink cans and some orange peel and sweet wrappers. And that was all it was. So I thought, *So what?*

I jabbed down with my thumb and a little flame appeared at the corner of the lighter.

A shadow just flitted across Daniel's face. That wasn't what he'd expected. A week ago I'd been too scared to hold the thing. And now —

There was a chip bag on the ground by my feet. I picked it up, held it by the corner between finger and thumb, and brought the lighter over to it.

I'd thought it would flare — expire in a flash, a blaze, an instant. But instead the plastic twisted, melted. I held it so the flames went up, up, away from my fingers, and I watched it burn.

Halfway through it burning I offered it to Daniel.

And he took a step away.

I think I smiled. I couldn't help it. And then, when the flames had eaten their way right to my fingertips, I dropped the ball of molten plastic and flattened it with my foot.

When it was quite out I threw the lighter back at Daniel — he wasn't expecting that, either, and he fumbled the catch — and then I went and took a place between Matt and Ben on the grass.

"I didn't know they burned slowly like that," said Matt, interested. "Didn't it hurt?"

I shrugged. I was watching Daniel: Daniel, who'd lost his power over me. How did that feel?

And then I saw his face.

And although it was still shining, I felt afraid.

45

Jack spent the rest of the evening seeing how many legs you had to pull off an ant before it started limping; Matt was nearly asleep; and Ben and me had nothing to do but watch Daniel and Ryan playing the slave game:

Sit, fatso!

Fetch!

Stay, dog breath!

Daniel could get Ryan to do anything.

"Be careful!" I said, without thinking, as Daniel tripped Ryan with a neat foot and sent him belly-flopping and gasping to the ground.

Daniel stopped and looked at me. Looked right inside me. I don't know what he saw, because I didn't know what was there myself.

"Why?" he asked.

"Because he gets asthma," I said, more or less at

random. And, of course, Jack started jumping round chanting, *Steve loves Ryan, Steve loves Ryan.*

I helped Ryan up. He started laughing again as soon as he'd got his breath, so standing up for him was all a waste of effort.

Daniel watched me. He had a strange expression on his face — triumphant, I suppose, or gloating: but I told myself he had no power over me anymore, and so I dismissed it.

As soon as Ryan was on his feet again, Daniel jumped up on his back and rode Ryan round the bench until he collapsed again in a wobbling, gasping, hysterical heap.

"You need a whip," said Jack, hopefully, as Daniel extricated himself tidily.

But Daniel flicked a speck of dust from his combats, shook his hair into its usual angel wings, and said something about having had enough of Ryan's smell.

I mean, Daniel: he had all that power, and he chose to use it like that.

Daniel the great.

Daniel, everyone's hero.

Tremendous, wasn't it?

We all went home soon after that, but I just

happened to look back as I was waiting to ride my bike out onto the main road. And there was Ryan, trudging home. And there was something about the set of his shoulders that reminded me of someone.

It wasn't until I was putting my bike away in the shed that I realized that he reminded me of me.

46

"Oh, no," said Mum, next day, when I got home from school. She was doing more washing — I think it must be a kind of compulsion with her. "I thought we had another box of powder. Stevie, do you think —"

I had no idea which bit of the shop they kept the soap in. I had to walk all round twice, and then to cap things I went and met Ryan at the cash register. It was really embarrassing being caught buying soap powder; but then Ryan was buying spray-on deodorant, so it was quits. We didn't really talk.

I rode home through the alley. I half noticed someone hanging around by the recycling bins, but I didn't really look. I suppose if I'd thought about it I might have made a guess at it being Daniel.

I saw Ryan coming out of the shop: lunge, lunge, like someone walking through soft sand. He should have got himself a bike — though his backside would have sagged round the seat like an over-risen muffin. His family were all inflated like beach balls: they could eat for England.

Families, I thought, hoping that no one would be able to see the box of soap through the bag. They were all so embarrassing — and you couldn't keep them quiet. There was Jack's mum — "All right, babe?" — and Ben's nan smelling of public toilets. No, you couldn't keep them quiet.

Unless, of course, you were Daniel. Daniel, the almighty. None of us knew anything about him. What *did* we know? He could drive a kart, and water-ski. His parents had loads of money. He'd been expelled from his boarding school.

What for?

I did know one thing about his school, now I came to think about it. Matt had said something once about a boy at Daniel's school who'd killed himself. He'd collapsed on the grass — of a drug overdose? Something like that. That was right, it'd happened just before Daniel left.

"Great. Thanks, Stevie," said Mum, as she opened the door.

"Yuck, what's that smell?"

"Oh, just sink-unblocking stuff. The silly thing keeps running slow. I'm sure I'm going to have to take it all to bits, but I'm giving it one last blast just in case."

"Stinky stinky sink-unblocking stuff," chanted Claire. "Stinky sinky stink-unblocking stuff."

I went up to my room to do some delicious homework, but for some reason — like the fact that it was mind-stuffingly boring — I couldn't concentrate on it. I kept thinking about Highford.

It was Ryan's fault. That glimpse of him had reminded me how I used to feel then: when everything was such an effort I spent my life wading through molasses.

I'd have to talk to Ryan. Daniel was so in love with himself he might get really nasty, really dangerous. It'd been bad enough yesterday evening when Daniel had been making fun of him in that blasted slave game.

What am I saying?

Fun?

Come off it. No one who walked home the way Ryan did had had fun. Daniel had been torturing him — he'd been torturing him for weeks. For heaven's sake, torturing *me* had only been a bit of variety for Daniel, a sideshow: but I'd been so busy cowering lovingly in front of him I hadn't realized.

Why hadn't I had the sense to see what was going on? I mean, I'd watched Ryan being humiliated again and again in front of all of us. And I'd always hated it, really, even when I'd been pretending I thought Daniel was cool to be so much in charge, so much in control.

Daniel had known how I felt. Yes, he'd known, long before I'd worked it out myself. He could look inside you and find out all sorts of things you didn't want to know. So he got double value from torturing Ryan, because he knew that he was torturing me as well.

Perhaps he was torturing all of us.

Oh, he was clever, was Daniel: he'd got it all worked out. He could show us what cowards we were, show us how badly we'd cope if he turned on us. Yes, he could get at any of us through Ryan.

And I thought of the way Daniel had looked at me; and I remembered the triumph shining in his face.

Triumph?

Downstairs Claire was still chanting.

Stinky sinky nose-unblocking stuff.

And then, in the black recesses of my brain, someone struck a match. And it flared, and it showed me something I'd forgotten I knew.

At Daniel's school: it wasn't drugs, it was sniffing

glue. No, not glue. No, that's right, it was aerosol. I remembered now. It'd happened just before Daniel left. Someone had died from sniffing aerosol spray just before Daniel got expelled.

And suddenly I saw everything.

Everything.

I think Mum called after me to know where I was going, but I was in too much of a hurry to answer.

47

I couldn't find them. I rode right round the shops twice, but I couldn't find them.

So I chained up my bike and went round again on foot.

What was — ?

Yes. Somewhere here, down the back alley: a murmur of voices.

Where?

Over here, over here. Behind the big supermarket bins. Up onto the pile of cardboard and —

And there they were.

They didn't notice me. I looked down on them and again I felt as if I was in the police helicopter that flies round and round the houses.

Ryan was lying back against the wall. For a long empty moment I thought I was too late: but the other person was talking to him, talking to him, gently, persistently.

You don't smell so much now. A few more lungfuls and that'll get rid of your dog breath.

The deodorant can was in Ryan's pudgy hand, but he was waving it sideways as if he wasn't sure where his face was.

And suddenly I was in a nightmare — so many nightmares — and I seemed to hear someone shouting, *That'll give him a proper haircut!* But even though I knew the voice was inside my head, was pretend, it was still there. And I couldn't move. I couldn't even speak.

And it was going to happen again.

I was in a nightmare, and everything was blinding bright, inky black, blinding bright; and fading, and fading.

And the world was moving, heaving under me. And I was falling.

Falling into the nightmare.

I landed soft. I suppose it must have been on Ryan.

All I know is that I hit something, and rolled, and ended up in a grazed tangle on the tarmac.

The shock cleared my head. And suddenly I was in the real world again, and that other time, when I'd been burned, was long ago.

I pushed myself up on one elbow. Ryan was still

holding the can, but his eyes were glazy. I don't think he knew what was happening. I snatched the can from him, pushed myself to my feet, and dropped it into one of the tall bins.

Then I turned to face Daniel.

Daniel looked at me, and his face was beautiful: beautiful, like an angel's. And my heart was thumping, because he was powerful and I was only me. I waited for him to make me worthless, make me powerless.

But as I looked at him I realized that I was taller than he was; taller, and somehow growing. And something inside me was making my fingers fizz.

But Ryan was coughing; coughing and wheezing and fighting for breath; so I turned to him.

And when I looked back Daniel was gone.

48

Matt's mum said Matt was busy with his homework, but she let me go up to his room. And Matt was doing his homework.

"But Ryan's all right?" he asked, suddenly fearful, interrupting the story.

There had been sirens, clashing, coming straight at me; but Ryan was all right.

"Did you tell anyone what happened?"

Sir, sir, it was all Daniel's fault, he started it.

That was no good. I knew it was no good because people had been told before.

"I need to know where Daniel lives," I said.

Matt blinked at me.

"What are you going to do?"

I didn't know.

"OK. I'll go with you."

Massive, Daniel's house was, with white pillars

holding up the porch, and stone lions, and a garden that went on forever. Somewhere someone was revving up an engine.

I dropped my bike in the middle of the drive and pulled the bell-thing beside the front door. We waited, but there was something about the hollow sound of the bell that told us the house was empty.

Matt stirred.

"He's there," he said. "Look, in the back."

Beyond the tangle of leaves that twisted through the trellis, there was someone on a kart. Someone slim, who drove fast, with style.

The side gate was no problem to us.

Daniel didn't see us until we were halfway across the lawn. Then he turned and drove at us just fast enough and close enough to make us run. Then he braked and let the engine settle down to a ticking and a purring.

"We've come about Ryan," said Matt: and Daniel came so near to smiling.

"I didn't touch him."

I suppose that was as true as most things are.

"We'll tell," said Matt, who didn't understand things like I did. "We'll tell every kid in the school. You'll be so sorry."

Daniel did smile then, as sleek and shiny as a cat that has been sipping blood.

"I'm not going back to school," he said. "My father has found a new school that'll take me — a proper school. He seems to think it will be a fresh opportunity: though, personally, I feel I'm managing things perfectly well as I am."

Together, I suppose, Matt and I could have killed him. Smashed his skull in with one of those stone lions. Strangled him with a bicycle chain.

Perhaps we would have. At any rate, Matt — or perhaps it was both of us — took a step towards Daniel as he sat in his shiny kart. But he laughed at us. Laughed in our faces, all smooth and shiny and perfect as he was.

And then he put his foot on the accelerator.

I should have got myself back over the gate, like Matt. But I wasn't thinking clearly — wasn't thinking at all, except about the heavy tires on the thing coming after me.

I was suddenly running across a vast desert of grass and the whining motor of the kart was close at my heels.

There was a steep bank in front of me with trees at the top, trees planted close together. If I could get up there —

Matt shouted something, but the revving of the motor chopped up the sound into blurting fragments.

I flung myself at the slope, snatching at the long grass, going fast, fast, with the whirring motor making the earth fizz under my fingertips.

And so I didn't see what happened.

But the motor sound changed — it got higher, and angrier, like a wasp in a barrel. And then there were two bumping thuds — one — two — heavy — but my feet were slipping and I had no time to wonder what it meant. I snatched at a bramble, never minding the hooked thorns.

And then there was a moment of silence — pure, clear, silence, like the beginning of the end of the world. And Matt called out, *Daniel!*

And there came a crash and a snap and a thud and a roar all together, and for a moment my heart stopped working.

And when I looked round, the tires of the kart were reared up facing me.

I couldn't see Daniel.

And he wasn't making any noise.

49

I went to the park on Friday evening. Sat on the bench and waited.

Ben came first, with Ryan. And we sat and couldn't think of anything to say.

Then Jack arrived with his hands in his pockets, and the silence became even more angular, filled with the sniggering jokes Jack should be telling. But even he didn't dare speak them.

Matt's face was thin. He hadn't bothered to change out of his school shirt.

We hung about and none of us could think of anything to say or anything to do.

"Did you have a good holiday?" asked Ben, at last, stupidly, like an adult. But I found myself answering him, telling him; anything to keep away the futile silence. I told them about the site — pretty pathetic, I said. And I told them about my family, and how I'd dragged round after them. And they listened, and they understood.

And then the silence fell again, and I couldn't stand it, so I said: *Look!* and I pulled something out of my pocket.

"Eurgh!" said Jack. "A slug! Steve carries a slug around in his pocket. That's sick, that is. Really sick."

"I found a big lump of cheese in my nan's pocket the other day," said Ben.

Matt poked the devil's toenail cautiously. Turned it over on my palm.

"What is it? A stone?"

So I told them what it was.

Jack, solid space from ear to ear, said:

"What's it for, then?"

And I thought, *What is it for?*

And suddenly everything was laid out in front of me like a hand of cards, and I saw it, and I understood it.

The devil's toenail was for changing me: for making me something I wasn't, didn't want to be. It was for turning me into Daniel. It was for destroying me.

I took it in my right hand and weighed it. Rubbed my thumb on it for the last time. And then, with a feeling as if I was opening a window, I drew back my arm and threw — threw as hard as I could. It sailed high, high into the air. Our eyes followed it, lost it against the leaves of an ash tree, and finally we heard it fall. Somewhere.

"You total prat," said Jack, blinking, dazzled by the sun. "That might have been worth something."

I didn't care because suddenly breathing was easier. Everything was easier.

"I saved my sister's life on holiday," I said.

Yes. That was something *I* had done. Not the devil's toenail, which was only pretend, but truly me.

"Really?" asked Ben, willing it to be true: willing it to be true so there were good things, as well as bad.

So I told them about it. Everything. The truth. How I'd wanted to do something to impress them. And how I'd failed. And they shifted about and looked sideways at each other.

And then at last Ryan said, "I reckon saving somebody's life is a lot better than just setting fire to a bin."

"Yeah," said Jack, just a bit reluctantly, after a pause. "I mean, saving someone's life. That's unusual."

And then they both looked at Matt. For approval.

"Yeah," said Matt. "All that arson stuff's boring."

"My cousin said the food in his detention center was rubbish," said Jack.

They all nodded, almost thoughtfully. Together. Well, they were a gang, weren't they?

I got up.

"Where are you going?" asked Jack, squinting up at me.

I didn't know: just somewhere different. Somewhere I wanted to be. Just for a while, probably: but I'd caught a glimpse of many things through that one window; and I wanted to look for them, because they were very bright.

"I'll see you around, OK?"

I was skimming away on my bike before they could speak. And I wasn't afraid anymore — not of anyone, not even Highford. They'd done their worst. But I'd survived. Body and soul. *I* had survived.

The sun was shining through the trees and everything was golden.

Life was precious. Oh, yes, just so precious.

Even mine.

This way, this way. In the long grass. That's right. Pick it up. It's spooky, isn't it? Enough to make you believe in my power.

Who are you?

Tom is half human, half elf...
and all on his own.

★ "ORIGINAL AND GRIPPING" —*Publishers Weekly*, starred review

COLD TOM

a novel by SALLY PRUE

SCHOLASTIC

Chased out of the elf world as a half-breed, Tom is running for his life. Though he can turn invisible to avoid trouble, he's still lost without his tribe. Then he meets Anna, a lonely human girl. Is her affection a trap, or will she help Tom find his true home?

SCHOLASTIC